ALSO BY
MATT WALLACE

BUMP

D1020264

SUPERVI
TO
FAT

THE SUPERVILLAIN'S GUIDE TO BEING A FAT KID

MATT WALLACE

WITHDRAWN

KATHERINE TEGEN BOOKS
An Imprint of HarperCollins Publishers

Katherine Tegen Books is an imprint of HarperCollins Publishers.

The Supervillain's Guide to Being a Fat Kid
Copyright © 2022 by Matt Wallace
www.harpercollinschildrens.com

Library of Congress Cataloging-in-Publication Data
Names: Wallace, Matt, author.
Title: The supervillain's guide to being a fat kid / Matt Wallace.
Description: First edition. | New York : Katherine Tegen Books, [2022] | Audience: Ages 8-12 | Audience: Grades 4-6 | Summary: "A young boy writes to an imprisoned supervillain for help after he is bullied relentlessly for being fat"-- Provided by publisher.
Identifiers: LCCN 2021024294 | ISBN 978-0-06-300803-8 (hardcover)
Subjects: CYAC: Bullying--Fiction. | Self-esteem--Fiction. | Superheroes--Fiction.
Classification: LCC PZ7.1.W3535 Su 2022 | DDC [Fic]--dc23
LC record available at https://lccn.loc.gov/2021024294

Typography by Andrea Vandergrift
21 22 23 24 25 PC/LSCH 10 9 8 7 6 5 4 3 2 1
❖
First Edition

For every fat kid who doesn't know how awesome they are.
Don't change yourselves. Change the world.

PROLOGUE

WHAT WOULD MASTER PLAN DO?

Max shouldn't have been thinking about revenge, about taking down Johnny Properzi once and for all. Max shouldn't have been thinking about how good it would feel to throw him through the nearest window. The boy the whole school called Johnny Pro had already gotten what he deserved for making Max's life miserable, at least that's what Max told himself. But to have Johnny Pro physically feel just a little of what he'd made Max feel since the school year began, what other kids like him had made Max feel for as long as Max could remember . . . that was so tempting.

He knew he could do it. He had the training now.

Max should have been thinking instead about finishing

the plan, about putting "the last piece in the puzzle," like his friend, teacher, and mentor told him he could do at this party. Revenge wasn't part of that plan.

That should have been at the front of Max's brain, but all Max could think about was how uncomfortable the suit he was wearing made him.

Master Plan said he'd get used to it. He told Max that it was like anything we do to help us become the people we want to be. Those things can be uncomfortable at first, they can even hurt, but it is the kind of hurt that's like a broken bone healing. In the end, it makes you stronger.

Most kids in the sixth grade didn't wear suits to school, at least not to his school. He'd told Master Plan that he'd get killed wearing one to class. But this was a party.

It was only the second time he'd ever worn one. The first was at his first Communion ceremony, and it was this itchy brown thing his mother bought at a secondhand shop that was too small. He remembered he could barely keep the shirt tucked inside the pants.

The suit Master Plan had ordered for Max, made just to fit him, was like wearing a cloud compared to that other one, but it was still more than he was used to.

Master Plan told him it was the last step in changing the way the other kids thought of him. Max did think the suit looked cool. He just didn't like it because it made him sweat. Everything made him sweat, but wearing layers of clothes always made it worse.

Max watched half the Captain Clobbertime Memorial Middle School Water Polo Team striding toward him, danger in their every step and fury in their eyes, led by the eighth-grade boy whose downfall Max had directly caused.

He wondered if he was sweating more because of the extra clothes, or because of how nervous he felt about what was about to happen.

Max had learned a lot since he opened his first email from Master Plan, but the biggest thing he'd learned was that there are things people do and say that they can never take back. There are some things that saying sorry for isn't enough. Those things change people and the world around them forever. You had to decide if doing them would change your world for the better, and if making that happen was worth it to you.

Master Plan was the one who had taught Max what "consequence" meant and, more than that, what it could do to people.

That's how Max knew that what he had done to Johnny Pro was one of those things you couldn't take back. As he watched the boy, the one who'd made him afraid just to exist, about to step to him, Max knew at once that if he let Johnny Pro provoke Max into acting, something else would happen that he couldn't take back. The world around him would change. And whether that change was good for Max, it would definitely be bad for the other boys.

A big part of him wanted that to happen.

He still wasn't sure, though.

Master Plan wouldn't wait. Max knew that. He wouldn't ask himself questions. He wouldn't be sweating through two shirts. Master Plan would've already decided to wreck them all if they were coming after him.

But Max wasn't Master Plan.

Yet.

A second ago, he didn't think he could sweat any more or any harder, but he was wrong.

LOWER CLASS

Max yawned until his jaw hurt. He could never sleep the night before the first day of school, and last night had been even worse. It was probably because he was starting at an entirely new school the next day, his first day as a sixth grader. He'd been among the biggest and oldest kids in elementary the year before, and now he was the youngest. He was far from the smallest but being big had never seemed to help him. It was the opposite, in fact.

He'd stayed up most of the night watching the same movie over and over again, *Waitress*, the one about the girl who bakes different pies and names them after all the problems she's having in her life. Those problems were a lot more adult than anything Max had dealt with, but he still liked the idea, and he loved the pie recipes. He'd made his own versions of all of them at home.

He wished he were in his kitchen now. At least he had Luca. The two of them were posted up outside on a cement bench in the quad of Captain Clobbertime Memorial Middle School, waiting for the first bell.

Max always felt weird thinking of Luca as his "best" friend, partly because Luca was his only friend, and partly because Luca had never said Max was *his* best friend. It also might have been because neither of them had really decided to hang out. They sort of just fell together a few years ago. In elementary school, kids made fun of Luca for wearing the same clothes almost every day, and they didn't always smell great. The same kids made fun of Max for being fat. They started eating lunch together, because they were the only ones who didn't make fun of them.

"Did you hear about Cobalt?" Luca asked him.

"No, what about him?"

"I dunno, I was asking you. They were saying something about him on the news when my mom dropped me off. It sounded like a big deal."

"Probably got another medal or blew up another building or satellite or something, and they have to pretend it wasn't an accident."

"Dude, that happened like *one* time. Why do you always

talk smack about him for that? Cobalt's the coolest."

Max ignored the question. He usually did when the subject of superheroes came up. He was also distracted, though. There was a girl across the quad who looked to be their age giving out cookies from a plastic container. She was just sort of handing them out to what looked like random sixth graders, smiling and laughing.

Her smile was nice. Her laugh, too. Neither seemed fake to Max. She was pretty, but it was the cookies that interested him. He wondered if she baked them herself. He didn't know any other kids who baked.

"Do you know her?" Max asked Luca.

"Who?"

Max didn't want to point, so he leaned his head in the girl's direction.

"With the cookies," he said.

Luca looked over at her without even trying to be sneaky about it.

"Dude!" Max barked.

He looked from the girl to Max, blinking.

"What?"

Max just shook his head. "Did she go to our old school?"

Luca shrugged. "Maybe? Like, in another class? I dunno."

"You think she made those cookies herself?"

"How would I know? Maybe? Why?"

"I dunno. They look good."

"They look good, or she looks good?"

"Shut up, dude. I'm not being gross. I just was . . ."

"You should go ask her if you're so curious. You bake, too. You could talk about it. We said middle school was gonna be different for us, right? Talking to a girl the first day would be different."

Max thought that sounded terrifying and impossible, not different.

He realized the girl was getting closer and closer to where he and Luca were sitting. Max's heart started beating fast.

"What is wrong with you, man?" Luca asked, staring at him like Max was slowly transforming into a large bug or something.

"What? Nothing."

The next thing Max knew, he was staring into the girl's open plastic container of cookies, and she was looking down at them on the bench.

"Hey, you guys went to Glow Girl Elementary, right?"

Max didn't say anything. Fortunately, out of the corner of his eye, he saw Luca nodding.

The girl nodded. "Yeah, I remember seeing you at recess. Here, I made cookies for everybody. I figured we all need it, y'know?"

"That's a cool thing to do," Max managed to say.

"Can I take two?" Luca asked. "I missed breakfast."

"Sure! You both can, if you want."

Luca quickly grabbed four cookies, handing two to Max.

"See you in classes, maybe?" the girl said to them, her eyes meeting Max's for a second before she walked away.

Max crammed most of the first cookie into his mouth. It tasted amazing. There were chocolate *and* peanut butter chips, and what he thought were vanilla chips.

"These cookies *rule*!" Luca mumbled with his mouth also full. "You should definitely get her recipe and make these."

Max only nodded. He still had his mouth full of half-chewed cookie, crumbs covering his cheeks and the front of his shirt like grains of sand, when several long shadows fell over him and Luca.

They were older boys, maybe even eighth graders. The three of them were wearing the same Capes jacket. The Capes were the school sports team name.

They did *not* look like they wanted to give Max and Luca free cookies.

Max knew right away and from experience that the tallest one standing in the middle of them was going to be the biggest problem. He had that look on his face. Max knew that look. While the other boys barely seemed to even see Max and Luca, the tall one was staring *right* at Max, like nothing in the world except Max even existed. His eyes were full of something that wasn't totally anger or menace, although there was plenty of both there. It was more like disgust, though, like whatever he was looking at was the grossest thing he'd ever seen.

"You're getting crumbs all over my bench," he said to Max.

"How's it your bench?" Luca asked.

Those mad, disgusted eyes snapped to Luca for just a second. "Shut up, thrift store, nobody's talking to you!"

The leader looked back at Max, as if he was waiting for Max to say something.

Max tried to chew faster so he could swallow the cookie in his mouth, but that only seemed to make the other boy angrier.

"God, you look like a cow when you do that. Stop it!"

Max stopped chewing.

"Can you even talk?" the boy demanded.

"His mouth's full, and you told him to stop chewing," Luca pointed out, only for one of the boy's teammates to reach down and flick Luca in the face with his fingers.

"I said shut up!" the tall one who was doing all the talking yelled at him.

Luca dropped his gaze to the ground.

"I asked you a question," the eighth grader said to Max.

Max didn't know what to do, so he did nothing.

That was the wrong choice, apparently.

The tallest one reached down and grabbed Max in a headlock, holding his neck tightly with one arm and pulling Max from the bench. Max lost his balance and fell to his knees. The older boy dropped to the ground with him, keeping ahold of Max and pulling up Max's shirt, over his belly. He started slapping him in the stomach as if he were using Max's belly to clap.

Max spit chewed-up cookie all over the grass as he cried out and struggled just to breathe. The other boy was strong. It was impossible to break free. Max could see Luca trying to help him, but the older boy's teammates kept pushing him down against the cement bench.

Max shut his eyes tight. It wasn't getting his belly slapped, although that stung mightily. It wasn't even that he had to gasp to breathe. He just didn't want to see everyone who was watching this happen. That was always the worst part.

When it was over and the eighth grader let him go, Max realized he'd started crying without even knowing it.

Max heard laughing. He didn't want to, but he opened his eyes. A big crowd had gathered, mostly upper-class kids. Through his teary eyes he didn't see a face that wasn't grinning or smiling, like this was the funniest thing they'd ever seen.

Then they started chanting like they were at a sports game cheering for their favorite player.

"Johnny Pro! Johnny Pro! Johnny Pro!"

What the heck is a Johnny Pro?

The boy who had just wrestled him to the ground stood over Max and raised his arms in the air like a rock star.

He must be Johnny Pro, Max thought.

The eighth graders were gone by the time a teacher, a ferret-faced little man with a mustache and wearing a whistle around his neck, pushed his way through the crowd to find Max barely managing to sit up on the ground.

"You want to be suspended for fighting on your first day?" the teacher asked him angrily. "Get up and get to your first class!"

Max could only blink his wet eyes up at the adult. He couldn't believe the man was yelling at him.

The teacher turned to the crowd that had gathered. "All of you, let's go! Now!"

He'd already forgotten about Max. He was busy herding the kids who'd laughed at Max from the quad.

Luca was there, on his knees next to Max. His hair was all messed up, and his cheeks were dark red.

He helped pull Max to his feet and tugged Max's shirt down over his swollen belly for him.

"Bad start, huh?" Luca said.

"Did the cookie girl see that?" Max managed to ask through a bout of coughing.

"I dunno, but we can just pretend she didn't."

Max's legs were shaking. He clenched and unclenched his hands, trying to breathe normally again.

The first bell that was really a beep finally came, sounding across the quad.

"Forget it and let's just go to first period, okay?" Luca said, trying to sound reassuring.

"Is middle school different yet?" Max asked his friend, laughing so he wouldn't start crying again.

SUPERHEROES SUCK, AND YOU KNOW IT

"**H**ow was your first day?"

It was the question Max had been afraid of hearing since he got home from school.

His mom never got home until very late in the evening, so Max had hours to think about it. He did his homework, feeling more than a little overwhelmed by being assigned work by multiple teachers instead of just one. He figured out what he was going to make them for dinner, as he often did during the week. He preferred baking, but Max was turning into a pretty good cook.

It was past 8:00 p.m. when his mom walked through the door of their apartment, tired as usual.

Max was sitting at the little bar counter between the

kitchen and the living room, reading a book he'd started at the end of summer.

She'd barely even put down her briefcase and said hello before she asked him.

"It's school," he said, not even trying to put on a smile. "It's the same as it always is."

His mom sighed, probably more because of the way he'd said it than anything. They'd had a whole talk over the summer (or rather, his mom had talked *at* him) about how Max needed to "try" more at school, to make new friends and try to find things he liked about his classes.

"Were the other kids nice, at least?" she asked, trying to sound hopeful.

"One girl gave out cookies she made to all the new kids, which was cool. And then . . ."

Max stopped, wincing as memories of what happened after that.

"And then?" his mom asked, waiting.

"Nothing," he said.

He just couldn't. He couldn't tell her about Johnny Pro.

Max knew it wasn't that she didn't care or didn't want to help, or even that she didn't listen to him. Mostly she was just busy. His parents had divorced when he was a baby, and his father had moved across the country. They never talked, and Max knew his dad didn't help them with anything. It was just his mom, on her own, and she had to work long, hard hours to make sure they had everything they needed. Most of the week he barely saw her.

A lot of the time he didn't want to make things harder on her with his problems. The rest of the time it just felt pointless. She couldn't *do* anything about it. She wasn't there with him during the day at school.

"Hey, maybe you could write a letter to Cobalt. I see him all the time on Facebook where he gives advice to kids."

"I don't really like Cobalt, Mom."

She stared at him like he'd just told her he didn't like french fries.

"What do you mean? Since when?"

"Since always."

"This is news to me," his mom said. "I always thought Cobalt was your favorite. You're always reading about him. That's why I mentioned it."

Max definitely wasn't going to tell her that the reason he liked Cobalt stories was because Cobalt's nemesis was Master Plan, and Max thought Master Plan was actually kind of awesome.

"Maybe you could write to another superhero you *do* like," his mom suggested.

"I hate superheroes," Max said before he'd really thought about it.

It was true, though. As far back as he could remember Max had hated superheroes.

His mom looked really shocked now. "Well, this is the first I'm hearing about it! How long have you felt like this?"

Max regretted opening his mouth, but for some reason he didn't want to take it back, maybe because of the day he'd had.

"I guess for a long time I pretended that I did. Whenever I was around the cousins, or around adults who were talking about the news and how some superhero did something all superhero-y or whatever, I'd just be like, 'Yeah, that's awesome. We're lucky they're out there.' But I don't think I ever meant it."

"Why not?"

Max took a deep breath, thinking about it.

"For a long time I didn't know. It even felt weird that I didn't love them like everyone else. But a couple of years ago I started thinking about how I was impressed at first, but then I started to notice stuff. Stuff other people didn't seem to talk about, like how superheroes always make things worse. Every time we'd see a news story about a big battle between a superhero and a villain, it was like the hero had wrecked a whole city trying to beat up the villain."

"That's not their fault!" his mom insisted. "They're not

17

the ones forcing some villain to commit crimes or . . . or hatch some nefarious plot that needs to be stopped!"

Max knew she wouldn't get it. He was sorry he'd even tried to explain it to her.

He thought part of it was that she'd never really had to deal with superhero fallout. They lived in a smaller town, and the big heroes only seemed to do their hero-ing in large cities. That was another thing that bugged Max, because bad things happened in towns like his, too. His mom and him had driven through Acropolis City once, on their way to his grandmother's, right after Cobalt had "stopped" Ragemonger from stealing something, a bunch of expensive jewels or whatever.

It took them two hours longer than it should have to go from one side of the city to the other. A huge part of Acropolis was closed off because of massive damage. Entire buildings had been smashed to absolute dust in the fight between Cobalt and Ragemonger.

It looked bad. Just seeing the wreckage scared Max.

He asked his mom who had knocked down all the buildings.

She told him Cobalt had done it to stop a bad guy.

Max asked why he had to knock down all the buildings to stop the bad guy.

She told him that's what superheroes did.

Max asked his mom if Cobalt was going to put the buildings back up.

His mom was quiet for a minute, and then she said she didn't think so, no.

Max asked his mom why not.

She said she didn't know.

Max asked his mom if anyone was hurt when Cobalt knocked the buildings down because she said he had to knock them down.

His mom told him they would get McDonald's cheeseburgers if he stopped asking her these questions.

Max thought about reminding her of that time, but he knew it would only make her *really* mad.

That was another reason why you couldn't tell adults anything, he decided. At least nothing real. They just wanted kids to listen to them and do what they say. They didn't want kids making them feel wrong, or like they didn't know something. They didn't want to have to rethink all the stuff they were so sure they knew already.

Max didn't understand how you could expect to teach anyone if you weren't willing to learn yourself.

"Anyway," his mom said, as happy to change the subject as he was, "what's for dinner?"

THE RACE

Max didn't know the kid's name. The only class they had together was physical education, and the two of them hadn't spoken to each other once so far. All Max knew about the other boy was that he was even bigger than Max, almost twice his size, especially through the middle, and he always wore sweater-vests. He had a different colored one for every day of the week, it seemed.

They started having their daily "race" that first week of school. Neither of them had agreed out loud that that's what it was, but they both knew they were racing each other at the beginning of fourth period every day.

PE was the class Max had been dreading the most going into middle school, and for one reason: he knew they made you change clothes for it. They'd explained the whole thing during orientation for fifth graders moving up. Each of them would be issued a set of gym clothes by the school and a padlock with a combination. There was a wall of tiny lockers, barely the size of cereal boxes, outside the school gymnasium. They were each assigned one in which to keep their gym clothes. Inside the gym, there were bigger lockers that were available for anyone to use.

At the beginning of PE class, they were to report to the gym, retrieve their gym clothes, and then pick an open locker inside the locker room to stash their books and backpacks and street clothes after they'd changed. They were supposed to use the padlock to lock up their stuff during class.

This is what scared Max more than anything about the sixth grade, more than moving to a new school, more than having so many different classes and teachers, more than the classwork getting harder, and, before he'd met Johnny Pro on his first day, even more than the seventh and eighth graders. He didn't want to change clothes in front of the other boys. He didn't want to change in front of anyone, ever. He even wore a shirt whenever he went swimming at a public pool or the beach.

The gym clothes were every bit as terrible as he knew they'd be for him, too. The shorts were okay. They were black and stretchy enough that they didn't look too tight on him, but the shirt barely fit him. It was white, too. He always thought wearing white made him look gigantic.

The boy's locker room wasn't that big, and half of it was a bathroom with sinks and just one stall with a door on it where the toilet was. When they had talked to the fifth graders about gym class, they'd specifically told them *not* to change clothes inside the stall. They told them not to be shy or nervous, because no one would be looking at them.

Max didn't believe that, and as soon as he saw the stall he knew if he was changing his clothes, it was happening in there, where he could be alone.

The problem was he wasn't the only fat kid in PE class. They were only given five minutes to change and get outside where their PE teacher was waiting. If you were late you got in trouble, and it happened in front of the whole class. Max found out the hard way on the second day of PE when the sweater vest kid beat him to the free stall. By the time he was done changing and shuffled out of the stall past Max, there were only a few seconds left before the start of class.

By the end of the first week of school, Max had started running between bells before PE. It really bugged Luca, who'd roll his eyes and yell at Max every time Max sprinted away from him in the hall after third period.

"You're going to give yourself a heart attack," Luca had scolded him. "If you just change real fast with everyone, no one will have time to mess with you."

They had PE different periods, and Max told himself, and Luca, it would be different if Max didn't have to do it alone.

They both knew that was a lie, though.

Max was so obsessed with making it to that open bathroom stall first so he wouldn't have to change in front of the others that he barely even noticed other kids making fun of him as he ran to the locker rooms. He couldn't explain, even to himself, why the thought of kids making fun of his body was worse than kids making fun of him for running through the halls, but to Max it was.

One day, as he hurried to get out of his street clothes and into his gym clothes, Max looked down and spotted the chunky fake leather shoes worn by his competition for the stall. He watched the feet inside those shoes shuffle from side to side, nervously and impatiently, waiting for their turn.

Max stopped changing suddenly. Something about the way the other boy was shifting his feet. For Max it was like looking into a mirror and seeing how scared he was. That made him feel bad. There were thirty kids out there

23

in the locker room who weren't scared or panicked right now. They were laughing and joking and having a good time before class. Max could hear them. He wanted to be out there, too.

He just couldn't, though. School was hard enough in the halls, dealing with Johnny Pro and the other seventh and eighth graders who wanted to make him their entertainment. He had to do whatever it took to make it through the day, to make things a little easier to deal with.

Max hoped it wouldn't always be that way, but he'd also had a lot of hope for moving up to sixth grade, and so far that hope had been smashed into the dirt.

REACHING OUT

The first few weeks of the school year dragged on slowly for Max, and he found that when he came home at the end of the day, he wanted to leave his house less and less. It was the only place he felt, not only safe, but removed from his trouble adjusting to life in the sixth grade.

He'd tried to shake off everything that had happened on the first day, but it was clear by the end of that first week that Max had managed to become Johnny Pro's favorite between-classes activity. It was like winning a contest Max hadn't even entered, and the prize was a big target painted on his back.

Sometimes it was an actual target. At lunch Johnny Pro and his teammates had started pelting Max with french fries from across the cafeteria. One such lunchtime, Johnny Pro even tried to make Max pick one up off the floor after it had hit Max in the face and eat it. The only reason Max hadn't ended up doing it was because a teacher wandered near them, not that they were really paying attention.

Every time they passed each other in the halls, Johnny Pro either shoved Max into a wall or spit at his head. If Max had to walk past them when Johnny Pro and his teammates were hanging out in the quad and they didn't feel like chasing after him, they'd just shout horrible names at Max or make sounds like Max's every step was causing an earthquake.

Max's troubles in PE class had made things worse, as well. Word had gotten around school about his refusal to change in the open locker room, and in addition to getting teased by many of his own classmates, even the eighth graders had heard about it. It gave Johnny Pro something else to torment Max about. His latest favorite thing was to tug at Max's shirt whenever he saw him, as if Johnny Pro was going to yank the shirt off in front of everyone. He hadn't done it yet, but the fear of it was almost worse for Max.

Max wanted to blame Johnny Pro's attention on the girl with the cookies, but he couldn't. She was too nice, and when he thought about her, anger was the opposite of what he felt. Max also knew it wasn't Johnny Pro seeing him eat a cookie that set the boy off. Max just existing would've been enough to do that, either way.

He'd tried talking to one of his new teachers, Mr. Spangler, about it, but Max couldn't figure out how to explain what was going on to him. It never sounded as bad as it felt when Max tried to put it into words, at least to him. He felt like Mr. Spangler would think Max was whining, or a tattletale, even though the teacher seemed concerned and ready to listen. In the end, Max just gave up.

Back at home, Max finished his homework, brushed his teeth, and went to his bedroom, shutting the door behind him. He didn't turn on the light. He liked the dark, most of the time.

He thought about what he and his mom had talked about after his first day of school. It wasn't that he liked the villains. He didn't want to be a bad guy. Max wasn't a mean kid. He felt sorry for people who had things worse than he did, and he knew there were a lot of them. He knew being fat and getting picked on a lot and feeling like nobody but his mom and his best friend liked him was far from the most horrible thing that could happen to a person.

That didn't make being that fat kid any easier, though.

In the same way, he just didn't think superheroes

actually made stuff better, at least not any of the stuff Max would have tried to fix if he could do what they could do.

Maybe that was what bugged him the most: thinking about what *he* could do with that kind of power.

It also seemed to Max like villains didn't just wear costumes and have nicknames. There were plenty of adults his mom talked about who sure seemed like villains that superheroes never seemed to do anything about. What good were they, then?

He'd only been a sixth grader for a few weeks, but sixth grade already seemed worse than a lot of villains he'd read about. The only thing he didn't hate about it so far was Luca and the girl who gave him the cookies. She and Max ended up having a couple of classes together. He'd been too embarrassed to so much as look in her direction, but he found out when the teacher did roll call that her name was Marina.

The rest of middle school sucked worse than superheroes.

Thinking about that gave Max an idea. Actually, it was that thought and something his mom had said earlier, when she suggested he write a letter to—*ugh*—Cobalt.

Max opened his laptop and did an internet search for Master Plan, the supervillain.

He wasn't sure what he was expecting (most supervillains didn't exactly have websites or social media accounts), but the top searches knocked him for a loop. There was a bunch of big news articles that had been posted a few weeks about him. Max wasn't expecting that. That must've been what Luca was talking about that first day of school. Cobalt had finally captured Master Plan several months back after Master Plan tried to blow up a factory that he said was polluting the environment and a nearby town. His trial had been dragging on ever since.

The news stories said that earlier in the week, Cobalt had testified against Master Plan in court, and the judge had sentenced Master Plan to life in prison.

Max couldn't believe it. He wondered why Luca had said the news was about Cobalt, but then it occurred to him that's why he always had to read stories about Cobalt to learn more about Master Plan. No one ever talked about Master Plan unless it had to do with Cobalt, and he was always the star of the story, the hero.

That really sucked, Max thought.

There was a picture of Master Plan along with the article about his sentencing. Max stared at it. He wasn't just a big guy, he was huge. Master Plan didn't have muscles that looked like they were carved from rock like a lot of super-heroes did, though. He was big like Max. He always wore really cool suits, and his hair was slicked back.

Master Plan was the reason Max stopped hating and being afraid of the word "fat." The supervillain had written a book that was one of Max's favorites. In it he talked about how there was nothing wrong with that word, or with being fat. It's the way people treat you when you are fat that's the problem.

Max found he felt sorry for Master Plan, really sad.

Then he thought even though it was sad, this turn of events could actually help Max with his own plan.

Max searched the internet for the prison the news said Master Plan was going to spend the rest of his life inside. He found they had a website. There was even an address where you could write to inmates in the prison, although in big bold letters it said anything you wrote to an inmate would be scanned and could be read by the prison.

That held Max up for just a minute, but he decided not to let it stop him. He wasn't going to ask Master Plan about anything illegal, after all.

Max grabbed his school backpack and unzipped it, taking out his notebook and a pencil.

His mom had been half right, he figured. Except he didn't need advice on surviving middle school from a superhero. He needed advice from someone who actually knew what he was dealing with.

Dear Mr. Marconius,

I know you hate being called Master Plan, so I
made sure not to write it in this letter or on the
envelope. I think I understand why you don't like
it. People have a lot of names for me I don't like
either. They have since preschool. I wouldn't want
to get a letter with any of those names on it.

I like your real name a lot. My name is Max, too.
Not Maximo like you, but my family calls me Max.
It's really Maxwell. Maxwell Tercero. I am eleven
years old. I just started sixth grade this year.

I don't mean to say I'm like you, or you are like
me. I know that's not true. I'm just a kid, and you
are you. I guess it just meant something to me. That
we kind of have the same name, and that you
are heavy like me. I hope me writing that doesn't
make you mad or make you feel bad. I don't mean
it as an insult. I have always been heavy, too. Fat.
I should just say fat. It is just like you write in your
book, there is nothing wrong with the word "fat" and
we should take it back from people who use it as an
insult.

I don't see a lot of fat people who are smart
and powerful and really do something about things

that are wrong with the world like you do. I read your book The Bad Guys. I read it twice, actually. I really love how you didn't take any money for the book and had the publisher give it to all those environmental organizations instead. But what I really liked was everything you wrote about Cobalt, how everyone calls him a hero even though it was him who wrecked half the city to capture you after you shut down that plastic factory, but you are the only one who is in prison from it.

I read a lot about petrochemical plants and all the terrible things they do to the environment after I read your book, and like you say in it, between you and Cobalt, you were the only one doing something to protect the people who live by that plant. It's like you wrote. "Be assured that Cobalt, the garishly costumed oaf, will not visit a single resident when the variety of illnesses caused by living beside that monstrous cancer-belching factory puts them all in hospital beds."

I never liked Cobalt anyway. He always sounds like such a poseur when they interview him.

I guess that is why I am writing to you. I know the same thing you know. How the people everyone thinks are the good guys so much of the time really aren't. We have a lot of those in my school. I have to deal with them every day.

I thought moving up from fifth grade, things might start to be different, but they are actually worse. The kids are bigger, and I feel like they are meaner and there are more of them. There's this one eighth grader. He's the captain of one of the school teams. He has already made me like his pet project of humiliation.

There is this girl in my English and math classes I keep wanting to talk to. Her name is Marina. But every time we have been out in the quad together or at lunch, I feel like the bigger kids pull something on me before I ever get the chance to say anything to her.

My school says they have a "zero-tolerance policy" for bullying, but it seems like what they think is bullying is a lot different from what I think it is. Whenever I have said anything to them, they just tell me I have to stop being so sensitive.

My mom tries. I remember when I was in second grade, she followed me to school without me knowing because she was afraid the other kids were giving me a hard time. She said she watched me sit alone at lunch and it made her sad. But her doing that didn't help anything. It is like she does too much and she can't do enough at the same time. Does that make sense?

I don't want middle school to be like elementary. I don't think I will make it another three years like that. But I don't know who can help me. I thought maybe you would have some advice. I know you are not like me now, but you were like me when you were my age, right? You didn't write a lot about that in your book, but from what you did write about when you were in school reminded me a lot of how I feel most of the time.

I don't want to do anything to hurt anybody. I'm not one of those kids. And just in case anyone else finds this letter and reads it, I want them to know that. We have lockdown drills at my school all the time, and every time we have to hide, my stomach twists up and I get these bad headaches. I would never be the person who makes that happen.

That's the other reason I wanted to ask your advice. You never actually hurt anybody that I know of. You just hurt things. And reading your book, I feel like maybe those things you hurt need to be gone. But you were always real careful never to kill or hurt an actual person.

So without hurting anybody, what can I do? I can't make school go away. I have to go.

Thank you very much for reading this, if they let you. I hope they do.

Sincerely,
Max Tercero

Mr. Tercero,

While I appreciate the sentiments expressed in your letter, and I do thank you for taking the time and care to compose that letter, it would be inappropriate for me to communicate with, let alone advise, a boy of your age, especially in the matters you discussed. I have only just begun my rehabilitation and wish to be a model inmate.

I strongly suggest you seek assistance from the proper channels, such as schoolteachers and administrators. They are there to help you.

I apologize for not being able to offer more from my current state of confinement, and I wish you good fortune in whatever comes.

Cordially,
Maximo Marconius III

TORN UP

MONDAY MORNING, FIRST BELL

Max had the letter in its plain white envelope carefully tucked inside his school folder. He'd been so disappointed when he first read it that he almost crumpled up the piece of paper and threw it in the trash. But he couldn't. It was actually written by Master Plan, to Max. Marconius was the most famous person he'd ever met, even if Max hadn't truly met him in person. Besides, what else could he have expected? Thousands of people probably write to someone like Master Plan. Max was probably lucky to hear back from him at all.

But he couldn't leave the letter in his room, where his mother might have come across it. He hadn't told anyone he'd written to Maximo Marconius III. His mom would've freaked out, probably grounded him for life. He hadn't even told Luca. It wasn't that he was afraid Luca would judge him; Max just didn't know how to explain to anyone else why he felt the need to send the supervillain that letter.

At school Monday morning, Max opened his folder, just to check that the letter was still there. As disappointed as he was, it was still the coolest thing he'd ever owned. After running a fingertip along the envelope's edge, he turned to the book report he'd been working on the night before. He'd barely finished it in time, and he was still nervous about handing it in.

All the worrying he was doing at least distracted him from how hungry he was. Max had given most of his breakfast to Luca, just like he'd been doing for the past two weeks, even though the other boy always insisted they split it evenly. Their school wouldn't serve Luca in the cafeteria anymore. They said he owed them too much money for breakfast and lunches he hadn't paid for. Neither of the boys understood how a kid who didn't have a job or any money to begin with could owe money to someone, let alone a school that was supposed to be free, but the whole thing was pretty low on the list Max kept in his head of all the things adults pretended made sense that clearly made no sense.

"You want me to read it for you?" Luca asked, licking

syrup and waffle stick crumbs from his fingers.

"No, it's fine," Max lied, feeling weird about the idea of his friend looking at the book report.

Luca just nodded. A few weeks ago, he probably would have kept bugging Max until he let him help, but since Max had been sharing his breakfast and lunch with him, Luca didn't seem to want to challenge him about anything. Max didn't like that, but he wasn't sure what to say or how to fix it.

"Oh, dude," Max said, very much wanting to change the subject, "did you watch *Baked In* last night? The new one?"

Baked In was Max's favorite cooking show. He'd given Luca Max's family's streaming service password so he could watch it at his house. That was another thing Max hadn't told his mom about.

Max wasn't sure how much Luca actually enjoyed *Baked In*, but he at least humored Max about it.

Luca shook his head. "I tried, but it kept freezing. I don't think our computer can play it right."

They had one computer at Luca's house, and it was a very old desktop his grandmother had bought them years ago.

"Oh. So come over after school. We'll watch it."

"You already watched it, though."

"I don't care. I'll watch it again. It's a good one. They give them, like, fast-food stuff they have to figure out how to bake into their desserts. It's wild. And I'm making chili in the CrockPot. Come over and eat and we'll watch it."

Luca smiled, just a little.

"Okay," he said.

They had different first-period classes, which meant the two of them went separate ways when the first bell rang a moment later.

"See you at lunch," Max said, his stomach already making noises, and these weren't from hunger.

Luca could see he was worried. It was the way he looked at Max. But just like with the book report, Luca didn't say anything.

Max knew his friend understood, but it still wasn't the same for him. They picked on Luca, too, making fun of his clothes and talking about how dirty he was, but a lot of the time they just ignored him. That sucked in its own way, Max knew, but he wished he could be invisible like that.

"Yeah, see you," Luca finally said.

Max reached into his backpack, digging past several back issues of *Cobalt* comics and pulling out a big, folded piece of construction paper. He zipped up his bag and shouldered it before unfolding the large rectangle. He held it between both of his hands as he walked between the first in the row of the long concrete buildings where all the classrooms were.

He'd been drawing the map for the past few weeks since his disastrous first day. It was playing *Shotokan Masters* that gave him the idea. You didn't last five minutes in that game unless you kept track of your map and where you were and what you'd learn running around the digital world. If you didn't, you'd walk right into a whole battalion of Ashigaru you'd forgotten about or get roasted by an elemental dragon whose lair you got to close to without noticing. The map was everything, and it kept you out of danger more than anything else in your inventory.

It was a map of the school, but not a map of where everything *was* in the school. They'd handed those out to sixth graders on their first day. His map didn't tell you where *things* were; it told you where *people* were.

It wasn't like a lot of movies Max had seen about schools. Every group didn't dress and look the same. There were plenty of little pockets of friends who could all have been put together based on the clothes they wore, or the music they listened to, or what they liked and what they talked about. You couldn't tell who a group of kids were or what they'd do just by looking at them.

The trick was knowing where everyone hung out and

which groups would leave you alone as you walked past them and which wouldn't. It took Max a few weeks and every word that meant "fat" shouted at him to really figure it out.

First bell was the toughest route to navigate, because before classes started, everyone had more time to get together in their favorite spots and there were a lot more of those spots to avoid. Max had marked the best route to his first class of the day as going around the library to avoid most of the buildings between where he and Luca ate breakfast and his homeroom. There were dumpsters back there that smelled like week-old lunch, so most of the kids avoided it.

That part was easy. It was a little harder once you got on the other side of the library and had to deal with the halls between buildings. They all had vending machines in front of them, and for some reason Max couldn't begin to understand all the groups that staked out the vending machines as their spot were pretty nasty. Maybe it was all the sugar from the sodas, although Max had read once kids acting weird because of sugar was a myth.

That's the part of his route Max was studying as he walked past the library. He had his face buried so deep in his map he didn't notice Johnny Properzi until he ran right into the towering jock. When Max looked up, all he could see was the big "CCM" patch stitched onto the chest of Properzi's varsity jacket.

Since their first meeting, Max had learned he was captain of the water polo team. They were a big deal, because they'd won more championships than any of the school's other sports teams. Johnny Pro's teammates liked to yell his name in deep voices as they stormed the halls of the school together like a pack of wolves, or when he held down a sixth grader and slapped his belly until it was red and raw. They treated him like a hero.

He was definitely one of the guys Maximo Marconius wrote about in his book.

At that moment, Johnny only had one other boy with him, a redheaded kid who looked old enough to be in college. Max recognized him as one of the other kids who'd stopped Luca from helping Max on their first day.

"You lost?" Johnny Pro asked, staring at Max's map with a look on his face like he smelled something foul.

Before Max could answer, Johnny Pro snatched the map from his hands. Max only just managed to let it go before it ripped.

The eighth grader turned it sideways and then upside down, examining it. "You looking for buried treasure or something?"

"It's . . . for class," Max lied.

"What class?" Johnny Pro demanded.

His friend grabbed Max in a headlock, holding him around the neck tightly. He moved fast for someone as big as he was. His arm was like the thickest part of a baseball bat, and it was immediately hard for Max to breathe.

It didn't hurt as much as when the older boy pinched Max's left cheek between his thumb and the knuckle of his pointer finger.

Max tried to push against the bigger kid's arm and back, trying to free his head, but it was useless.

"He's like one of those bulldogs on Instagram," the boy laughed, squeezing the meat of his cheek until tears stung Max's eyes.

They all loved doing that to the fat kids, he noticed. It was like every dumb, mean kid on Earth had a meeting and decided that pinching a fat kid's cheek was going to be their official greeting.

Johnny Pro quickly got bored trying to figure out Max's map. That was one good thing about them, Max was learning. They got bored with everything fast, including messing with him.

Unfortunately, being bored didn't mean they just walked away. Johnny Pro tore Max's map into half a dozen shreds and dropped them to the ground.

"Watch where you're going, tubby," he instructed Max,

already looking past him like Max had stopped existing.

His friend, however, was still amused by Max wriggling.

He only stopped when Johnny Pro shouted at him to hurry up, saying they were going to be late again.

A few seconds later, Max was all by himself, staring down at the ripped pieces of his map, sucking back tears that had nothing to do with his stinging cheek or aching neck.

At least there was no one else around, no one to laugh at him or, even worse, watch him quietly with a disgusted look on their face.

Max picked up the pieces of the map, carefully stacking them together like a deck of cards. He could draw another map. The red, swollen, pinched skin of his cheek would flatten out and change back to its normal color. The stuff happening inside of him lasted longer. He knew later that night he'd lie in bed and think of all the things he should have done and said to them, clever burns that would make them have to hold back tears. He'd replay what just happened in his head, only he'd come out the winner.

Doing that always helped a little, but it never lasted long.

From: 8mevojd@lightservice.net
To: maximus928@gmail.com
Subject: From One Max to Another

Hello, Maxwell. Though you will not recognize the address from which this email has been sent to you, hopefully the subject line will compel you to open it.

Thank you again for your letter. I apologize for responding the way I did. The prison authorities read all my ingoing and outgoing mail, so I had no choice but to dissuade you when I wrote back.

I have hacked into the prison's server and am using it to send you this email, without anyone else reading it. Without those prying eyes, we can communicate honestly, and I can attempt to be of help to you in your present situation. I took the liberty of tracking down your email address as well. I hope you don't mind.

You were not wrong about our similarities. I was very much like you when I was your age. I was husky, afraid, frustrated, and clearly more intelligent than my peers. More than anything else, I felt powerless. It is, I believe, one of the worst feelings we experience as people, especially young people.

Your assessment of violence as a response to your troubles is entirely correct, and I commend you for that. Violence is far too often the tool of the wicked, and a lazy tool at that. It should only be used to defend one's life when that life is threatened and there is no other escape available. The means of inflicting violence on a large scale is too easily available to people your age. This is one of many issues I plan to address, in my own way and by my own methods, when I am free of my current confines. I digress, however, to the matter at hand.

The good news is you do not need violence to solve your problems. Be assured that your enemies are far, far weaker than you believe yourself to be. Were they not so weak and unsure, they would not need to inflict pain on you in order to feel better about themselves. They also suffer from a tragic lack of imagination. This can and will be their downfall.

I require a more detailed analysis of your situation, your opponents, and your goals. Only then may we begin to formulate an appropriate plan of action. Please reply with a breakdown of the worst offenders at your school, who they are, what their tactics are, and how they go about doing what they do.

I will help you resolve this matter. Us gentlemen of size and intellect must stick together, after all.

I look forward to hearing more from you.

Cordially,
Maximo

FOR YOUR EYES ONLY

Max read the email in the morning before school, and he wanted to fake being sick just so he could stay home and answer it, or at least think for hours about *how* to answer it.

At first he was certain it had to be a joke, a prank, but no one in the world besides Master Plan and the prison knew he'd written that letter, and Max couldn't believe anyone working at a prison would want to mess with him like this.

Besides, it just *sounded* like Master Plan. That was Maximo Marconius III's voice. There was no faking that. Max knew it.

That whole day went painfully slow, but it was also

a total blur. Max barely heard anything anyone said to him at school. Every time Luca tried to talk to him, Max spaced out after the first few sentences. Even Marina saying hi to him in English class couldn't distract him from thoughts of what was waiting for Max on his laptop when he got home.

Luca wanted to hang out after the last bell of the day, but Max told him he had chores to finish before his mom got home. He'd feel bad about lying to his friend later, but at that moment, if we waited any longer to read Master Plan's email again and begin working on his reply, Max thought he would explode.

When he was finally back in his bedroom, in front of his laptop, Max reread the words of Maximo Marconius III at least half a dozen times. Each sentence felt perfect to Max, like the man understood everything he'd been trying to say in his letter.

When he had memorized practically every word, Max clicked on the "reply" button and lowered his fingers to the keyboard of his laptop.

They stayed there, not moving.

He had no idea what to write, even though Max had spent the entire day thinking about nothing else. When it came to actually putting it into words, one after the other, he didn't know where to start.

He could tell Master Plan about Johnny Pro, and about everything he and the water polo team had done to Max since school began.

He could tell Master Plan about all the bullies before them, in elementary school.

He could tell Master Plan how he wanted to talk to Marina every day but didn't know how and didn't think a girl who was nice to everybody could actually like him.

None of that seemed right, though.

Max didn't know why. Those were all just things that happened. They weren't what really bothered him. They were like sneezes when you get a cold. They sucked, but they weren't what actually was making you sick.

Finally, Max decided he would try to tell Master Plan what being Max every day felt like. Maybe it would come out as a mess, a nonsense jumble of words, but starting that way felt right to him.

From: maximus928@gmail.com
To: 8mevojd@lightservice.net
Subject: What it's like

I have been trying to figure out how to explain to you what it's like for me at school, like you asked me to do. Did you ever feel like you were two different people when you were my age? Because there is the me when I am alone and there is me when I am at school around all the other kids.

I feel like I have to remember other kids don't see me the way I see me. When I think about myself, in my head I am not the fat kid. In my head, I am just like the rest of them. But that is when I am alone, with nothing and no one to remind me that is not true.

You know how a cereal company or a shoe company or whatever will have a contest? They make ads that tell you how you can enter and what you can win. But you have to be eligible. "Eligible" means only certain people can enter the contest.

It's like that at school with the other kids. I'm not eligible to them, for anything. Fat kids in dumb clothes their mom makes them wear are not eligible to hang out, to join in things, to be invited to parties or sleepovers or whatever. They decide I am not eligible without even talking to me.

That is what it is like. That is what I want to change.
It is not just being beat up or made fun of. I want that
to stop, too. But I want them to see me as eligible, just
to be one of them. I want Marina to think I am eligible.

Does that help?

—Max

Subject: RE: What it's like

Maxwell,

I am impressed by the way you describe how you feel and how
your classmates treat you. It is very much like not being eligible
to participate in your own life.

I felt as you did once, I promise you. I overcame that feeling
and changed my situation. You will, too. You will learn that you
have to make your own rules, Maxwell. In life you decide your
own eligibility.

This is very important, so please pay close attention. Do
not blame others. Do not blame girls for not wanting to talk to
you. No one owes you their time or their attention, Maxwell. You
deserve to be treated with respect. You do not deserve to be
bullied or insulted. You do, however, have to earn the respect
and affection of others, and it is up to them to give it or not give
it to you.

I can help you stop the bullying. I can help you deal with
those who treat you like a victim. I cannot, however, make girls
like you. No one should be "made" to do that. They have to
decide to like you and socialize with you. All you can do is
present your best self to them and ask them for what you want.

That is what I will help you do. Once you do that, you have to accept the decision others make about you. If they decide you are not their cup of tea, so to speak, then you must respect that and move on.

Your more immediate problems are the bullies. You cannot be or present your best self to others if you are living in fear every day. That is unacceptable. So we will deal with that first, and we deal with it swiftly.

I strongly dislike bullies.

Cordially,

Maximo

From: maximus928@gmail.com
To: 8mevojd@lightservice.net
Subject: Johnny Pro

His name is John Properzi, and everyone calls him Johnny Pro, which is such a dumb nickname, but everyone acts like it is so cool and he is an eighth grader and he is the captain of the school water polo team, which is a big deal because they have won all these championships, and he looks like he could be in college and he is the biggest tool I have ever met.

He likes to use me as a punching bag. But like really. He will just start teeing off on me, punching me all over. It doesn't ever really hurt that bad, I guess. It is not even about that, though. He likes to do it in front of his friends or some girl he likes, because he thinks it is funny or they think it is funny.

The other guys on the water polo team give me a hard time, too. They will grab me in headlocks or pinch my cheeks or push me into doors. But Johnny Pro is the worst one. He is always the one who starts it. They all look at him like they are dogs waiting for him to tell them what to do and pet them on the head.

I have never done anything to him. I don't think he even knows my name. It is like they held a meeting when school started, and they all looked at who was coming into the sixth grade and they picked me to be their punching bag because I'm the fat kid. He loves to make fun of me for being fat, too.

I just don't get why being fat makes them come after you like they do. What difference does it make to them if I am fat? What makes being fat a bad thing? If they all want to lift weights in the school gym and never eat a hot dog for lunch so they can look like Chris Evans I don't care.

Anyway. Johnny Pro is my biggest problem, like you said. I don't even want to hurt him. I just want him to leave me alone. And I feel like if he did then the rest of his squad would leave me alone, too.

—Max

From: 8mevojd@lightservice.net
To: maximus928@gmail.com
Subject: RE: Johnny Pro

Maxwell,

You may find as you grow older and see more of the world outside of your school that people and how they behave do not make much sense to you. This only means you are smart and aware, and they are neither of those things.

People are often afraid of anything or anyone who is different from them. People do not like being afraid. It makes them feel powerless. So instead of fear they choose anger. They choose to be angry at the thing or the person who is different for making them feel that way.

That same fear is at the root of why people of size are so often treated poorly by others, especially groups of other people, for seemingly no reason. From the time we are born, movies and television and online media teach us that there is only one type of body that is acceptable to have. That is part of it.

Too many kids your age and younger are taught by parents and other adults that if someone is fat it means they have no self-control, that people of size are weaker or less intelligent than someone else simply because that other person is thin. This is, of course, ridiculous.

All of this is about other people and their failings. It is not about you.

What you must understand about a boy like this so-called Johnny Pro is that he is less of a problem than the rest of your classmates. They are the ones who give him the power to do what he does by laughing and doing nothing to stop him.

Your classmates prop up Johnny Pro and allow him to treat you as he does for one of two reasons: They fear him, or they want to be him.

What we must do is take that fear away and change how they see him so that the last thing they ever want to be is a person like Johnny Pro.

In a Hollywood film, you would of course overcome him in a one-on-one battle and win the respect and admiration of your classmates.

In the real world, our world, physical violence will often only make the matter worse. That may seem an odd thing for someone who has been incarcerated and branded a "supervillain" like I have to tell you, but it is the truth.

Even if you were able to defeat him in a fight, it would earn you, at best, a week or two of peace. After that, with his pride wounded, he would come for you even more violently.

You have read my book and are a student of my work, so you know that I abhor physical violence. I also find it a terrible tool for accomplishing most goals.

The so-called "heroes" I have faced off against are not

all that different from your school bully. They are all totally convinced that they are better than you and that they have the right to use physical violence to solve anything they think is a problem.

To a superhero, there is no problem that cannot be solved by picking up and throwing a car at that problem. To your school bully, you are that problem. He keeps himself appearing strong by making you appear weak.

I have always found it best to use my superpowered opponent's own ego and weaknesses against them. They occasionally get lucky, as Cobalt did when he captured me, but there is usually nothing more dangerous to those kind of people than themselves.

Are you familiar at all with old cartoons, particularly Looney Tunes? There are two characters who come to mind, the Coyote and the Roadrunner. The Coyote is constantly pursuing the Roadrunner across the desert, devising all manner of ways to trap or exterminate him. The Coyote's plans always blow up in his face. The Roadrunner never "fights" him.

The man who drew many of these cartoons was a brilliant artist and storyteller named Chuck Jones. He established a set of rules for making Coyote and Roadrunner cartoons. Some of the most important rules are as follow:

- The Roadrunner cannot harm the Coyote except by going "meep, meep."

- No outside force can harm the Coyote—only his own ineptitude.
- The Coyote could stop anytime—if he were not a fanatic.
- The Coyote is always more humiliated than harmed by his failures.

Do you see how the Coyote is like your bully? If you do, then you also see how we will defeat him. You will take no direct action against him. You will allow his own failures and mistakes to be his undoing.

Like the Roadrunner, you will stay on the road. That's the Roadrunner's nature, the thing that makes him what he is. We must never go against our own nature.

All you will do, my young friend, is expose your bully for what he is.

To do this, I will have to advise you to suffer further humiliation at his hands. I am sorry for that. Like all the advice I will give you, it is your choice to follow it or not. If what I am about to suggest is too much for you, I understand. We can try something else.

If you have the courage for it, though, I believe we can solve your most pressing problem and change the way your other classmates see you in the process. . . .

CAUGHT ON VIDEO

The Amazon package was waiting on the doorstep when Max got home from school the next day. It was addressed to him, Maxwell, and not his mom.

He didn't know how Master Plan knew Max would get to the package before his mom, and maybe Max should have been at least a little freaked out by how much Master Plan seemed to know without Max telling him (Maximo was, after all, a supervillain who was in jail for trying to blow up a bunch of stuff, and he also tried to kill a famous superhero like every month when he wasn't in jail). Max also knew his mom would melt all the way down if she knew about any of this, even though, he told himself over and over, he hadn't actually lied to her about anything yet

61

(not telling her wasn't the same thing, he figured).

Max was nervous about all these things, but he couldn't make himself be afraid of them. He was too excited.

If he was scared of anything, it was what Master Plan had told him to do—not "ordered" or "instructed" him to do—just advised him to do. Master Plan was clear about that.

Inside the package was a video camera, a GoPro. It was the smallest camera Max had ever seen. It would be even less noticeable than a phone. It was easy enough to operate, the footage it recorded looked just like a movie, and he could upload it to his mom's laptop with no problem.

He took the GoPro to school with him the next morning. There was a half-circle bench of concrete in the quad where he always sat with Luca before first bell. He gave Luca his breakfast, because Max wasn't hungry. In fact, he felt like if he tried to eat anything he'd throw up.

Luca was talking to him about the latest episode of *Baked In*, where they gave the contestants different kinds of barbecue sauce to figure out how to make birthday cakes with, but Max wasn't really paying attention. He was looking around the quad, waiting to spot Johnny Pro.

He was starting to get nervous thinking the bell would ring, and he'd have to try again during lunch. He had to wait so close to the bell to do this, because Mr. Talbot was on quad duty in the mornings. Max had noticed he always left a few minutes early to get a snack before classes began. It seemed like he'd taken forever to go that day, but Mr. Talbot was finally gone.

Max didn't want to wait any longer. He'd spent all morning psyching himself up to do this, and now that he was at school, he just wanted to get it over with.

Thankfully (or maybe not so much, considering what Max was about to do), Johnny Pro appeared on the quad seven minutes before first bell. He posted up with a couple of his teammates and some girls near the wall of Building One, only a couple dozen feet from where Max and Luca were sitting.

It was time, and Max had to make it happen now. Max took a deep breath and let it out slow, balling his fists and then stretching his fingers. It helped distract him from how weak his legs felt and how much they didn't want to stand up or walk right then.

"What's wrong with you?" Luca finally asked him.

Max sneakily took out the small camera and set it next to him on the concrete slab. He aimed it across the quad where Johnny Pro was standing and started recording.

"I'm gonna do something that will look really weird and dumb, but after you can't ask me why I did it, okay?"

Luca stared at him.

"Huh?"

"Just . . . you'll see. Just sit here. I'm doing it for a reason."

Max got up and left the concrete circle, walking slowly across the quad toward where Johnny Pro was talking to his friends. He could feel Luca watching him the whole time, not understanding what was happening, or what was about to happen.

This is a bananas thing to do, Max told himself. *He's going to murder you.*

He didn't stop moving, though.

In fact, he started walking faster, almost jogging in a straight line toward the one kid he always tried to avoid.

At the last second, Max almost didn't do it. He felt a burning in the back of his throat, and something fizzing on top of his brain, and a voice inside his head screamed at him to run away.

Instead, he leaned his left shoulder forward and stepped right into the middle of Johnny Pro's back, bumping him between the stitched letters on his water polo team jacket.

The eighth grader turned around and roughly shoved Max against the wall behind him. Johnny Pro did it out of reflex more than anything. Max could see the older boy didn't actually recognize him until after he hit the wall.

"Dude, do you just suck at walking, or what?" he asked.

He didn't wait for an answer, or really want one. Johnny Pro socked Max in the upper part of his right arm, hard. Max felt it all the way down to the bone. He opened his mouth in pain but didn't actually make any sound.

Johnny Pro's friends laughed. That was all the encouragement he needed. Johnny Pro raised both of his fists and began punching Max in the chest and shoulders and stomach, fast and not as hard as the first shot he'd thrown, but hard enough to make Max shrink against the wall and try to turn away from the blows.

"Why can't you just leave me alone?" Max managed to squeak out through his tears and the fists flying at him.

"Why can't you stop eating?" Johnny Pro shot back at him.

Max could feel tears in his eyes, but he didn't stay quiet. "Why are you such a jerk all the time? Why do you only go for kids smaller than you? Are you scared to fight people in your own grade?"

He'd never questioned the older boy before during one of these beatings.

Johnny Pro didn't like it.

Suddenly the fists were coming at Max harder and faster and angrier, and it started to hurt more, until Max forgot all about the GoPro and about the plan concocted by a famous supervillain.

"Stop it!" he yelled, covering his face with his arms tightly.

Johnny Pro kept yelling, "Do something, then! Do something!"

Max could hear the bully breathing hard now. He felt Johnny Pro's spit, hot and wet and sticky, hit Max's face as Johnny continued to growl at him. He couldn't understand why the older boy was so mad, but the punches hurt, a lot. Johnny Pro wasn't playing anymore. He was really trying to mess Max up.

Just when Max was ready to scream, the punching stopped. He heard someone else yell, loud, and it was a voice much higher than Johnny Pro's.

Luca was between them. Max's friend was bent over with his arms around Johnny Pro's waist, trying to push him away from Max, yelling at him to stop.

Johnny Pro grabbed Luca and threw him to the ground. He kicked the smaller boy in the hip, and Luca cried out in pain.

Max stumbled forward. He was sore and hurting all over, but he was out of breath more from how upset he felt than getting punched by Johnny Pro. He fell as much as he dived to the ground, trying to crawl over Luca, to protect him from the eighth grader's attack.

But Johnny Pro didn't kick or punch them anymore.

The older boy was standing over them, just looking at the pair with big, angry eyes, his mouth wide open.

He looked like a totally different person than the one Max had bumped into.

Nobody watching was laughing anymore. The scene had stopped being funny. Everyone could feel how serious the whole thing had gotten.

Max could see it in their faces. They didn't know how to feel or what to do. They knew this wasn't okay. They knew Johnny Pro was out of control and shouldn't be hurting anyone like this.

But he was still John Properzi, the most popular kid in school, and Max and Luca were still sixth-grade scrubs nobody knew.

Johnny Pro finally looked up and noticed how they were all staring at him, even his friends. It snapped him out of whatever furious trance he'd gone into.

A few seconds later, he walked away from them like nothing happened.

Max tried to catch his breath. He could still feel at least a dozen spots on his body where Johnny Pro tagged him, and he knew he was going to have a bunch of ugly bruises the next day.

"You okay?" he asked Luca, sitting up on the ground.

"I'd ask why you did that," Luca said, sounding like he

was in pain, too, "but you said not to."

"I'm sorry."

"You're buying me lunch."

"Okay."

They helped each other to their feet. Luca was limping a little from Johnny Pro kicking him when he was down.

"What the heck is going on out here?!"

They both turned their heads toward the confused and angry adult voice. It was Mr. Talbot. There was a red-stained napkin tucked inside the collar of his shirt. He was holding a half-eaten jelly doughnut in one hand. Some of the filling was still on his chin.

No one answered him. All the kids who were still in the quad either walked away or looked at their shoes like they couldn't see or hear him. He didn't even seem to notice Max and Luca. He just knew there had been some kind of commotion, and he was too late to see what happened.

Then Max remembered the camera. He stumbled back across the quad and checked it. The GoPro was still recording. It had captured everything.

He'd gotten exactly what Master Plan wanted and probably a lot more than either of them expected.

Max just hoped it was worth it.

From: maximus928@gmail.com
To: 8mevojd@lightservice.net
Subject: Video

Here is the video.

                                          —Max

From: 8mevojd@lightservice.net
To: maximus928@gmail.com
Subject: RE: Video

Maxwell,

This was unpleasant to watch. I can only imagine how unpleasant it was for you to go through. I am sorry for that. But I am proud of you. You carried out our plan perfectly. You are much stronger than you give yourself credit for.

Do you know why he became so angry when you started asking him questions? It was not because you were defying him or challenging him. It was because you made him think, for the briefest second, about what he was doing to you. You made him think about you as a person. Bullies do not like that. If they are forced to remember that you are a person just like them, it means they have to consider that they are wrong, that they are cruel.

He was not angry with you. He was angry with himself.

In a way you gave him a chance. You gave him a choice. He could have chosen in that moment to stop. He could have chosen to treat you like a person, with respect.

Instead, he chose violence.

He will now have to pay for that choice.

We are going to make Johnny Pro famous, and not in the way

he might like to be. It is easy to ignore the bullied as a group. It is much harder to ignore it when this kind of cruelty is shoved directly into your face.

It is easy enough to make that happen. One just has to understand how the internet works. Everyone who runs a website or posts things on the internet is fighting for the attention of the public. To do this they need content. They need new content every hour of every day, or they lose that attention. It is far too difficult to create all this content by yourself, so they are always looking for the next viral story or picture or video to help keep the attention of their audience.

With your permission, I will post this video to a social media account I will create, posing as an upperclassman from your school. I will then send that link to as many of the people I just described as possible. I will not identify you or your friend who gallantly came to your aid. I will, however, identify this bully of yours.

We will see how cool your classmates think John Properzi is a week after this video has been shared across the entire world, and everyone who sees it calls him out for being the needlessly cruel young man he is.

Cordially,

Maximo

NOTED

Max had come to believe that having math class so close to the end of the school day should be illegal. Like, really, actually illegal. He wanted the police to come to his class and arrest their math teacher for trying to put probability facts and functions in their heads after 1:30 in the afternoon.

He was imagining that very thing happening, in fact, instead of focusing on his worksheet, when he saw a small hand reached past his arm from the seat behind him.

Marina's seat.

Her hand was holding a folded piece of paper. She was trying to be sneaky about it, Max could tell. It still took him a few seconds to accept that she was trying to pass *him*, Max Tercero, a note.

She'd never done that before.

Max hesitated, but he finally reached out and took the little triangle of paper from her hand. He kept his fist cupped around it, hiding it as he brought it to the middle of his desk. He started unfolding it over his worksheet, watching their math teacher to make sure he wasn't looking in Max's direction.

It wasn't a long note, just a couple of sentences. She had nice handwriting, though, not sloppy like his.

The note read, *I'm sorry about what happened to you and Luca in the quad. Are you okay?*

She wasn't in the quad when he'd intentionally bumped Johnny Pro and sparked off the fight (it was easier to think of it as a "fight" than a humiliating beating). Max probably couldn't have gone through with it if Marina had been watching. She must have heard about it from her friends. The whole school had been passing around garbled versions of the story since first period, and most of them weren't even true, from what Max had heard.

At least, judging by her words, Marina had been told something closer to what actually went down.

He picked up his pencil and wrote underneath her words, very carefully because he didn't want her thinking his penmanship sucked: *Yeah, just some bruises. I should have hit him back more.*

The "more" was definitely stretching the truth, as holding his arms up over his face didn't really count as "hitting back," but Max couldn't help it.

He refolded the paper, trying to follow the creases she'd made in it so that it became the perfect triangle Marina had made.

He looked up to see their math teacher staring at the screen of his phone.

Max dropped the note over his shoulder.

His heart started beating fast as he waited for Marina to write back, if she was going to write back.

He really hoped she would.

Max actually began counting seconds in his head. When he'd reached seventy-eight, he felt something pointed tickle the back of his neck, and it made his body go stiff.

He reached behind his head and touched the spot where he felt it with his fingertips.

Marina had tucked the note inside the collar of his shirt.

He thought he heard her giggling behind him. It was muffled, like she was keeping her hand pressed against her mouth to stop it.

Max couldn't believe it.

Is this flirting? Is this what flirting is? Is she flirting with me?

No, he told himself. *Don't be dumb. She's just being funny.*

Max pulled the note down from his shirt collar, again unfolding it and spreading it out over his worksheet.

This time what she'd written was even shorter than before, and she didn't say anything about Max's lack of offense in the "fight."

Her second note read, *Johnny Pro is such a . . .*

And then she wrote a word Max's mom would have grounded him for saying out loud, at least in front of other people. Marina had written the word all in capital letters and put a bunch of exclamation marks after it.

She'd even underlined it.

Max laughed out loud.

It was more of a giggle, but in a quiet room it might as well have been a gunshot. Everyone, their teacher included, looked up from what they were doing.

Max put a hand over his mouth and stared straight down at his desk, his cheeks turning as red as the blood inside them.

"Everybody should be *working*," their teacher said to no one in particular.

He clearly didn't mean himself, Max thought, but he was happy not to get busted.

Eventually the rest of the class had gone back to their worksheets. Max glanced over his shoulder, nervously.

Marina wasn't looking at him, but she was grinning down at her desk and he thought she was trying not to laugh. He didn't feel as embarrassed as he had a second ago, though.

It looked like she thought what happened was funny, and not that *he* was the joke.

That made Max smile.

He turned his attention back to the note on his desk, trying to think of what else to write her. He wanted to make her laugh with his words instead of him embarrassing himself.

Before he could come up with anything, however, the bell rang.

"All right!" their teacher announced. "If you didn't finish your worksheet, just take it home with you and have it done for the beginning of class tomorrow."

Max felt disappointed. It was the first time in the history of the world a sixth grader didn't want math class to end.

He didn't get up, though. Everyone around him did, packing up their stuff and shuffling out the door as quickly as they could, but Max thought he should turn around and say *out-loud words* to Marina.

He still couldn't think of anything, though.

Max decided just to go for it. He'd turn around, and whatever came out of his mouth, he'd make it work.

That's a terrible plan. You are terrible at planning things and you should feel bad about how terrible you are at it and definitely not do this plan especially.

Whatever, he told himself, ignoring the fact he was starting to sweat, a lot. *I'm going for it.*

He wiped his suddenly damp forehead and rubbed that hand on his pants. Max took a deep breath, and then he turned at the waist and put his arm on the top of the desk behind him, putting on what he hoped was a not-creep smile.

Marina was already gone.

The smile faded from his lips. Max was disappointed but also kind of relieved.

Still, a part of him was scared that short exchange with Marina was the only one he'd ever have.

She left their shared note behind. Max turned back to his own desk and looked down at it, his writing sandwiched between her writing.

He carefully folded the note back up, again trying to follow the same lines that Marina had made. When he was done, he tucked it inside his pocket.

"You need something, Max?" his math teacher asked him.

Max realized he was the only kid left in the classroom.

"Oh," he said. "No, I'm going."

He started loading his backpack, trying to hurry so he wouldn't be late for last period.

You need something?

Max thought about that question the rest of the day.

From: 8mevojd@lightservice.net
To: maximus928@gmail.com
Subject: Your Abilities and/or Skills

Maxwell,

Now that we are close to putting our little video project to bed, as it were, I would like to speak of something that is vital to the next part of our work together. So far we have focused too much on the negative. We have discussed what you do not like about yourself and your life, and what you are not good at when it comes to school and dealing with other people.

I would like to hear about the opposite side of that. I would like to hear about the things you are good at, that you do like.

Your instinct may to be to answer that you are not good at anything. I want you to stop and think about that.

Everyone has abilities and skills, Max. We do not always give ourselves credit for them, because often they are things that other people don't think are worthwhile.

I am here to tell you everything you are passionate about, everything you care about, is worthwhile.

Tell me what you are good at. Tell me what you enjoy, no matter how small you might think it is.

This is and can be, like all information, *very* useful if you know how to take advantage of it.

And I can show you how to do that.

Cordially,

Maximo

From: maximus928@gmail.com
To: 8mevojd@lightservice.net
Subject: RE: Your Abilities and/or Skills

I am good at some stuff. I'm pretty good at writing. I don't mean handwriting. My actual handwriting sucks. You saw it. But English is my best class.

I'm also pretty good at cooking and baking, way better than my mom anyway. I wouldn't tell her that, though. She does her best. But she can only make four things and it is like she has never heard of spices.

I like cooking. It's probably one of my favorite things to do. It takes my mind off things. So does writing, but that feels more like work. Cooking and baking are just fun.

My grandma taught me a bunch of stuff in the kitchen before she died. She didn't make a lot of different things either, but what she did make was awesome. She had a recipe for chicken cacciatore that is still the best thing I have ever eaten, and her peanut butter chocolate chip cookies were the best. I have tried to make them myself, but they are never the same.

I wish my grandma had taught my mom more. Dinner around here can be really depressing unless I make it.

I don't ever talk about it at school, because cooking isn't cool to the other kids. They don't have any classes for cooking or baking at my school either. My mom asked, but they told her that those programs had been cut a long time ago.

I don't really know how that can help us here. I can't bake a cake or make tacos for Johnny Pro. I mean I could, but I feel like he would probably just laugh at me and smash whatever I made him in my face. I guess I could make something for Marina, except even thinking about doing that makes me start to sweat. I would probably pass out before I could hand it to her and smash the food in my own face.

—Max

From: 8mevojd@lightservice.net
To: maximus928@gmail.com
Subject: RE: Your Abilities and/or Skills

Maxwell,

Being skilled at the culinary arts, cooking, is no small or humble feat. Having the power to feed people, and feed them well, is a truly great thing. Food is rare in that it is art as well as being a life-giving thing. Chefs are artists as well as scientists, and what they create affects people deeply in many ways.

There was a time in my life, when I was around your age in fact, that I did not believe I was good at anything of value to the world, let alone anything that was "cool." Then I realized I was good at something that could help me achieve anything I set my mind to achieving: I was good at understanding people. Why they do the things they do, what they want, what they will do in any situation based on who they are. I also understood how I could use that information to defeat anyone who opposed me.

That is also both an art and a science.

I shall have to factor your abilities and skills into our future plans. It will take some thought, but trust me, your culinary gift will be *very* useful to us.

We will come back to this. In the meantime, thank you for sharing this information with me.

Cordially,
Maximo

BEING SEEN

Johnny Pro beating up on Max and Luca was talked about throughout school for the rest of the week, but when everyone came back the following Monday, it seemed like they were all ready to move on to more current gossip. Max was okay with that. He didn't know how Master Plan was putting their video project "to bed," as he'd written, but the whole experience was so weird and humiliating that Max almost didn't care anymore.

He definitely didn't expect what happened next.

At first Max thought the other kids were staring at him because he was stuffing his face with the soggy waffle sticks they served for breakfast at school three days a week.

He was saving half of what he got from the cafeteria for Luca, who was late arriving that morning, and he noticed a group of girls from his social studies class watching him and whispering to each other. One of them had their phone out, and she was showing its screen to her friends.

Max tugged at his T-shirt, worried it was bunching against his fat rolls and that's what they were looking at.

He didn't even notice Luca finally walking up to him until his friend dropped down on the concrete circle.

"Those girls over there are watching a video of us," he said, snatching up a waffle stick and dipping it in the plastic cup of syrup.

"What? What do you mean?"

"They're watching a video of Johnny Pro jacking us up last week."

"Watching it where?"

Luca shrugged. "YouTube, I think? And that seventh grader over there is looking at it on TikTok. Did you know it went viral?"

He didn't want to lie outright to Luca, so Max didn't say anything.

"It's pretty messed up," Luca went on. "Properzi looks like a total psycho. You don't really see your face a lot in it, though, so I wouldn't worry. You don't see mine, either. But whoever recorded it got a *sick* angle of me shooting on

Johnny Pro. That was some UFC stuff. I could totally be a cage fighter."

"He threw you on the ground and kicked you like a soccer ball."

Luca looked more than a little offended.

"I mean, yeah, but I still looked good. Before that happened."

Max wiped his sticky syrup fingers against his ugly red pants, remembering how he'd told Luca to sit where he was when Max bumped Johnny Pro, and how Luca had tried to help him anyway.

"Hey," Max said. "I didn't, like, tell you thanks for jumping in like that."

Luca shrugged off the idea.

"You're my boy, right?" he said.

"Yeah, I am."

Luca grinned. "Then don't worry about it."

They finished their soggy breakfast and were waiting for first bell to ring when a voice came over the school PA system, booming across the quad.

"Max Tercero, please go to the vice principal's office before first period. Max Tercero, you are wanted in Vice Principal Dorazo's office."

"Uh-oh," Luca said.

"I didn't do anything," Max said.

"Yeah, go with that. I'll bet she never hears kids say that to her."

Max narrowed his eyes at Luca.

"Shut up."

Luca laughed. "Good luck, man."

Max left him to lick the remains of the syrup from its plastic cup.

When Max arrived at Vice Principal Dorazo's office, the door was open and Johnny Pro was already sitting in one of the chairs in front of her desk.

"Come in, Max," the VP said to him, waving him toward the empty chair.

Johnny Pro didn't look at Max right away, but as Max slowly lowered himself into the seat beside his tormentor, Johnny Pro flashed him a glance that could have melted ice. He was silently warning Max not to say anything.

Vice Principal Dorazo was barely four feet tall, but there wasn't a kid in school who wasn't scared to death of her. She had what Max heard other kids describe as "abuela energy."

She didn't look happy this morning, either.

The VP placed a tablet screen on her desk, the screen facing them both.

"This was just brought to my attention, and I am extremely disturbed by what I see here."

Luca was right; it was the video Max shot of Johnny Pro beating the pee out of them. Max hadn't watched it when he got home that day, at least not all of it. He had checked to make sure he and Johnny Pro were both in frame, and then turned it off before uploading it and attaching it to an email and sending it to Master Plan.

His stomach knotted as he watched Johnny Pro getting madder and madder and hitting him harder and harder. The worst part was when Luca charged in and tried to tackle the older boy. Seeing his friend get hurt trying to help him was worse pain than any of the bruises Max had ended up with later.

Something managed to distract Max from the disturbing replay of what happened. The video was playing on an internet web browser page. It wasn't just on Vice Principal Dorazo's hard drive. Someone had posted the video on an actual website, just like Luca had said he'd seen on their classmates' phones.

He did it, Max thought, trying not to let his real feelings show. *Master Plan actually did it*.

"This has been posted all over social media," the vice principal informed them. "At least five news blogs that I've seen have done stories about it. None of these stories are favorable toward you, Mr. Properzi, for obvious reasons. They are also not favorable toward our school for allowing this to take place."

Max didn't look straight at him, but from the corner of his eye, he could see Johnny Pro staring at him hatefully.

"John, do you have anything to say for yourself?" Vice Principal Dorazo demanded more than asked.

He shrugged. "We were just playing around."

"And?" she pressed.

"Things just got out of control, that's all."

The vice principal looked at Max.

"Max? Is this true?"

He just nodded.

The small woman frowned at them both. "I am not happy, boys. Neither is Principal Jones. Our school has a zero-tolerance policy when it comes to bullying. Which a lot of these . . . *blogs* make a point of saying."

"I wasn't bullying anybody," Johnny Pro insisted. "We were just playing. The other kid took it wrong. I got mad when he jumped on me. I didn't mean to hurt him. Besides, they're both fine now. Look at him."

It made Max feel sick to hear Johnny Pro lie like that, but he had to remind himself that getting the bully in trouble with the principal's office wasn't part of the plan. The whole point of shooting the video the way he did and Master Plan sending it out was so that nobody, including Johnny Pro, could blame Max for it getting around. If he ratted out Johnny Pro now, the other boy would only blame him more.

Besides, it wasn't about the adults. It was never about the adults. It didn't matter what they thought of Johnny Pro or Max, or what they did or tried to do about the situation. All that mattered was what the other kids in school thought, and what they did. That's all that ever mattered. The teachers never seemed to understand that, or at least they all acted like they didn't.

"Max?" the VP asked.

"I'm fine," he said.

She didn't look like she believed him, but Vice Principal Dorazo didn't press him any harder.

"John, you're captain of our water polo team," she said. "Other students look to you as a leader, someone to admire, to take after. I expect much more from you than this."

"Yes, ma'am," Johnny Pro said automatically.

"And, Max, if you have a problem with another student, especially an upperclassman, I expect you to come to this office and tell me, okay?"

"Yes, ma'am," Max said, also automatically, and just like Johnny Pro, he didn't mean it.

"You can both go to your first-period classes for now. I'll be reviewing this matter further with Principal Jones."

Excused, they both got up from their chairs and walked out of the VP's office.

"Be happy you kept your fat mouth shut!" Johnny Pro hissed at Max when they were far enough away from her door.

Just as he had in the office, Max chose silence.

He met up with Luca again in social studies class. After the bell, he told his friend everything that had happened in the VP's office.

"So you didn't say *anything*?" Luca asked, and he sounded confused.

Max shook his head.

"Why not? You could have nailed him! They probably would've kicked him off the team, or suspended him, or . . . I dunno, *something*!"

"And then he would've killed me. And you, probably."

"But . . . but . . ."

"The Coyote can only harm himself," Max said.

Luca blinked at him in silence. "Why do you sound like the inside of a fortune cookie all the time lately, man?"

"Never mind," Max said.

"So what happens now, then?"

That's a good question, Max thought, but he didn't say it out loud.

From: 8mevojd@lightservice.net
To: maximus928@gmail.com
Subject: Self-defense

Maxwell,

As we have discussed previously, I very rarely agree with using physical violence as a solution to any problem. It is, more often than not, the wrong tool for the job.

Unfortunately, as you have witnessed, those we have issues with, like bullies, or superheroes, usually don't agree with that.

It is regrettable the school has taken no action against young Jonathan. Fear not, I have a plan for that, one that will hopefully take care of several of our current problems all at once.

Until then, it is entirely possible, despite our best efforts to keep the blame off you, that he will seek some form of revenge against you for what he has suffered. I would like you to be better prepared to defend yourself, should he, or his friends, attack you.

Below you will find an address. It is a school not too far from where you live where an old acquaintance of mine teaches the art of self-defense. He is very skilled. You will have to tell him that I have sent you there, and you should also remind him that he owes me a debt.

Your mother, of course, will not want you training to fight

other children, whether they are bullies or not. You may tell your mother that your physical education teacher has a friend who has just opened a martial arts school, and any of their students who apply will receive three months of free lessons. If she believes this has a teacher's support, she will be more open to the idea. And I suspect your mother will be overjoyed that you are showing an interest in some form of after-school physical activity.

I am offering you this help on one condition: What you learn from Gunnar you are to use only to defend yourself, if another person, child or adult, physically attacks you. Our goal here is to free you from bullies, not turn you into one.

Cordially,
Maximo

GUNNAR'S
SELF-DEFENSE ACADEMY

His mom drove him to the school on Saturday afternoon. It wasn't hard to spot. There was a big sign above the front door that read GUNNAR'S SELF-DEFENSE ACADEMY with a picture drawn on it of a man with a long blond ponytail punching a board that had split clean in half.

"What kind of self-defense does he teach, exactly?" his mom asked.

"Karate, I guess? Our PE teacher didn't say, or maybe he said and I forgot."

"Well, it's good for health and discipline and focus and all that, I suppose."

"Right," Max said.

They walked inside just as a class seemed to be letting out. About a dozen kids of different ages, some as young as Max, others who looked like they were in high school, were all walking out with their gym bags and backpacks, many of them wearing martial arts uniforms (a gi, Max thought it was called).

The oldest, and only, person left in the room had to be the teacher. He was standing in the middle of a soft blue mat that covered almost the entire floor of the school.

Gunnar was a tall man with long blond hair that he kept tied in a ponytail, just like the image on the sign outside. He didn't wear a gi. Instead he was wearing simple black training pants and a black T-shirt with the Academy logo on it.

There were chairs by the door that had probably been placed there for visitors to watch the classes and wait.

"Mom, is it cool if I talk to him by myself? At least to tell him why I'm here?"

His mom smiled, like she was proud of him for trying to take control of the situation and be on his own.

"Sure, honeybun, go ahead. I'll be right over here."

He wanted to ask her not to call him that, *especially* here, but he could never seem to work up the nerve.

She settled down into one of the chairs and waited. Max walked away from her, grumbling to himself.

"Should I, like, take off my shoes?" Max called to Gunnar from the edge of the blue mat.

The self-defense instructor smiled at him.

"Thanks for asking," he said. "Please do."

Max slipped out of his shoes and left them behind, walking across the protective mat to meet what would hopefully be his new teacher.

"Can I help you with something, young man?"

Max opened his mouth to say hello and explain why he was there, but seeing Gunnar's face up close distracted him.

"Problem, son?" Gunnar asked.

"I just . . . I feel like I've seen you before."

"I have ads. In the penny-saver thing that comes to your house in the mail, with all the coupons."

"No, it's not that."

Max studied the man's face, thinking hard.

Then he tried imagining the man in a suit like Master Plan would wear, and suddenly it hit Max.

"Oh, dude. You were Master Plan's henchman!"

The smile left Gunnar's face. He cleared his throat loudly, looking over the top of Max's head at where Max's mom was sitting.

She smiled and waved at him.

Gunnar waved back. He smiled, too, but it didn't look to Max like a happy smile.

"First of all, kid," Gunnar said quietly, "I don't know what you're talking about. Second of all, 'henchman' is a very offensive term. The proper term is 'villainy aide,' okay?"

"So you were his villainy aide?"

"Yes. I mean no! *No*, I was not."

"You *totally* were. You were called 'Machine' something. Oh, I remember. Machination. You were called Machination."

"Oh god, I always hated that name," Gunnar groaned.

"I remember the news clip where they showed Cobalt kicking you in the junk so hard that you threw up all over Master Plan's shoes."

"That was a *cheap shot*!" Gunnar insisted, raising his voice. "I wasn't even looking!"

Gunnar stopped himself because he saw Max's mom look over at them curiously.

He smiled and waved reassuringly at her again.

Gunnar, or Machination, knelt down to look eye to eye with Max.

"Okay, look, I left that life behind, you understand? I have a new life, a new name, and a new identity. I am no longer associated with supervillainy of *any* kind. I'm just trying to run a square business here using the only legal skill I have."

"You mean fighting?"

"Self-defense," Gunnar said, speaking slowly like Max wasn't all that bright.

"Well, that's why I'm here, to learn self-defense. Master Plan is the one who sent me."

Gunnar wasn't expecting that. But instead of looking surprised, he looked like he just plain didn't believe Max.

"Wait, what? He did not."

"He did."

"He did *not*."

"He did. He said to tell you that you 'owe him a debt.'"

All the color drained out of Gunnar's already white face when he heard that.

"How . . . how do you know Master Plan?" he asked, whispering now. "Is he secretly your dad, or something?"

"No. He's just . . . my friend. He helps me."

"And that's how he helps you? By sending you here?"

"Yes."

"And he said that? That I owe him?"

"Yes."

"He used those words exactly?"

"Yes."

"Why does he want me to teach a little kid how to fight?"

"I'm not a little kid. And he just wants me to be able to defend myself. I'm having some problems at school."

"Yeah, you look like you'd have problems at school."

Max frowned, thinking that sounded a lot like an insult.

Gunnar sighed. "All right, okay, I'll show you a few things. That's it. But private lessons ain't cheap, kid."

"He said you wouldn't charge me."

"He what?!"

"Something wrong?" Max's mom called to them from the bench by the door.

Gunnar immediately smiled and waved at her politely.

"Nope! Nope, not a thing! Just teaching Max the, uh, academy fighting . . . chant."

"Three months of free lessons," Max told him, and because it had made Gunnar so afraid, he repeated, "He said you owe him."

"Yeah, yeah, I heard you!" Gunnar whispered, annoyed. "Okay, fine."

Max grinned.

"Cool."

WHERE THERE'S SMOKE, THERE'S FIRE

One Wednesday changed everything.

It was lunchtime. It had only taken a few days for the viral video of Max and Luca's battle with Johnny Pro to hit a million views online. On his way to their usual spot, Max overheard some of the bigger kids from the water polo team talking. They were saying Principal Jones himself pulled Johnny Pro out of his second-period class. Nobody knew why, though.

Max was eating with Luca when one of the largest men he'd ever seen in real life walked into the cafeteria. It was impossible not to notice him. Max thought at first it must be someone's dad, or maybe a substitute PE teacher or a new football coach.

Then, at every table, it seemed like, kids started to gasp and yell out in surprise and excitement.

Max looked around in confusion, and then he studied the adult he'd never seen before more closely.

"Dude, is that . . . ?" Luca began to say, and then stopped dead when he was suddenly sure he saw what Max and the rest of the kids saw.

Max couldn't believe it. The gigantic man in their cafeteria was The Smoke. It was really him.

The Smoke was one of the hottest new superheroes in the world. He was in movies. He had tens of millions of followers online. Max saw other kids wearing his image on their T-shirts almost every day. It helped that he was ridiculously handsome and charismatic and that he looked like a bodybuilder, Max guessed.

Personally, Max thought he was a joke. He had the power to turn himself into actual, real smoke, and then he could make the smoke change colors or make words or different objects or even imitate people or animals—but made from smoke.

He was useless. That's what nobody ever said, except for trolls on the internet, and Max didn't get it. It seemed impressive, sure, until you realized smoke can't do anything. It can't touch anything. It can't stop bullets or knives or bolts of energy. It can't even stop a bank robber from running away. There were entire compilation videos on the internet of criminals running right through the smoke, usually set to some kind of funny music.

Still, The Smoke was super famous and loved by millions. There was no denying that.

There was a whole crew of people following behind him with cameras and what looked like recording equipment from a movie set. They were filming him.

Luca was ready to leap out of his chair next to Max.

"What . . . ? Why would he be *here*?"

Max could only shake his head.

Then he started thinking about what Master Plan had written to him about the internet. The Smoke did a lot of charity work, and one of his big ones lately, Max knew from reading his Twitter feed, was a thing called #AllInTogether. It was an anti-bullying campaign The Smoke had started that was supposed to bring kids in every school together to stop anyone from being beat up or harassed. He posted videos to his Twitter and Instagram all the time where he went to different schools and talked to kids who'd been bullies, and the bullies themselves, making them apologize for what they'd done and make friends with their victims.

At least on camera.

He usually ended his visits by transforming into the campaign's hashtag, made out of smoke.

"Is he looking at us?" Luca asked excitedly. "I think he's looking at us!"

"Oh god," Max muttered to himself.

"Hey!" The Smoke called out, and he pointed at Max and Luca's table. "Those are two bad hombres whose faces I recognize!"

His voice was deep and booming, and he flashed a smile at them both that had the most teeth Max had ever seen in a regular human mouth.

That's when it hit Max.

The Smoke was talking about them.

He strode over to their table, towering above them like a skyscraper made of muscles.

"You're Max, right?"

"Uh, yeah."

"And this is your boy, right? Your wingman?"

"Luca," Max managed.

The Smoke offered Max his hand to shake.

Max took it, or tried to. The Smoke's hands were huge. He could've crushed Max's entire head in just one of his fists.

He shook Luca's hand, too. When he was done, Luca looked at his own fingers like they were made of solid gold.

The Smoke stood tall and turned to address the entire cafeteria.

"I want everybody here to know how much I admire Max and Luca. Just like you, I'll bet, I saw the video of them being pushed around by one of your bigger classmates. They stood up for each other. That's not easy, especially when it's an older kid, somebody who is popular and cool and looked up to by your classmates."

The Smoke got more a serious look on his face. His voice grew a little softer but still loud enough to be heard by everyone and no less commanding.

"I want to say something else, and I'm not calling anyone out by name here. I believe you're all good kids. But I'm going to say this straight up: Y'all need to take better care of each other. And when I say 'each other,' I mean *everybody*, especially your younger classmates like Max and Luca here. They deserve to come to school in a safe place. All of y'all deserve that, okay? I know it's hard for y'all. Believe it or not, The Smoke was a kid once. Only I was never little. My pop used to call me Doughboy."

Everyone laughed like that was the funniest thing any adult had ever said in the history of saying funny things.

Max didn't laugh. He couldn't believe someone like The Smoke was ever a fat kid like him.

"And before I discovered my powers, boy, did other kids love poking fun at The Smoke."

Everyone gasped at that, like such a thing was unthinkable. Who would dare provoke one of the world's greatest heroes and his fearsome powers of setting off smoke alarms?

"Remember, you're all in this together. Love each other. Take care of each other. It doesn't take guts to pick on people smaller or weaker than you. Real guts is treating everyone with respect, and saying something when you see something. Now . . . CAN YOU SMELL . . . THE SMOOOOOOOOOOKE?!"

That was his signature catchphrase, the one he ended all his interviews with on the news whenever he distracted a criminal long enough for someone else to bring them down.

The entire cafeteria exploded in cheers and applause.

He high-fived Max and then Luca.

"I've got some officially licensed The Smoke shirts and hats for you guys, okay? Let me just go do a quick wrap-up for the cameras there and we'll hang."

"Sure, yeah, we'll hang," Luca said quickly, like this was something that happened to him every day.

Max looked at his friend like Luca had just thrown up a hive of bees.

"Did that just happen?" Luca asked him after The Smoke had walked away to talk to his video cameras.

The rest of the day passed in a weird blur that Max barely noticed.

He knew the T-shirt The Smoke gave him wouldn't fit,

but Max didn't say anything.

Luca said it was the nicest thing he'd ever been given as a present.

Johnny Pro wasn't in school the next day. Max and Luca found out he'd been suspended from school for a whole month, and that he was off the water polo team.

Max guessed not even The Smoke could convince Johnny Pro to apologize to sixth graders, on camera or off.

By lunch everyone was watching the video The Smoke had posted across all his social media accounts, the one of him visiting Max and Luca at school, praising them, and giving his speech.

He hashtagged every post #AllInTogether.

A couple of days later, one of Johnny Pro's teammates, the one who'd held Max in a headlock and pinched his cheeks, came up to him between classes. Max thought the tank-sized jock was going to pound him into the ground to get revenge.

Instead, he asked if Max could get him The Smoke's autograph.

MOMENTUM

"Did the boss . . . I mean, did Master Plan ever give you that whole talk about using your opponent's weaknesses against them?" Gunnar asked Max at the beginning of their first lesson.

They were alone in Gunnar's school after his last class of the afternoon. Max was worried the Academy wouldn't have a gi that would fit him, but Gunnar told him to just wear loose clothes that he could move around in.

"Yeah, he did," Max said.

"And letting them harm themselves instead of you harming them. All of that?"

"Yeah, like the Roadrunner and the Coyote."

Gunnar grinned, but it wasn't a nice grin.

"He always loved using those corny old cartoons to make his point. Anyway. That same idea works for defending yourself when somebody comes at you. That's why he hired me as his villainy aide."

"Henchman."

"Villainy aide," Gunnar repeated, grinding his teeth as he said it.

Max wanted to laugh, but he stopped himself.

"Anyway," Gunnar went on, "what I'm going to teach you I learned from this Russian dude I shared a prison cell with for a few years."

"What did you do that they sent you to jail?"

"I said a bad word," Gunnar told him, clearly lying. "Now, pay attention!"

Max straightened up, making a serious face and listening closely.

"This is called Systema. One of the big ideas of Systema is you don't use force to throw people around. You use their natural momentum. You know what momentum is?"

Max had heard the word before, but he had a tough time thinking about how to explain it, so he just shook his head.

"Think of it like this. A guy jumps at you. When he's moving through the air, coming toward you, that's his momentum."

"Okay."

"I'll give you an example of how it works."

Gunnar stepped behind Max, kneeling down so that their heads were mostly level with each other. He reached out and put one hand on Max's side and the other on his shoulder.

"Now, step back and wrap your arm around mine. Don't try to hold me, just press your arm against your own body and let that trap my arm."

Max looped his arm around Gunnar's, not really holding it, just flattening it against the side of Max's body.

"Okay, now, *don't* try to pull me around. My arm is trapped between your arm and your side here. You got me. You don't need to use force. Instead, just turn your body to the left, and then drop to one knee."

Max nodded and spun himself to the left, bending his leg and going down to one knee at the end.

As he did, Gunnar's arm was pulled along for the ride, and it caused the rest of the instructor's body to fall over Max and to the mat below. Gunnar landed on his back, looking up at Max with a small smile.

Max wasn't sure if Gunnar *let* him do it, but it definitely didn't feel like Gunnar was fighting back or trying to stop him.

Still, Max was surprised by how much power and control he felt.

"You see? You're not using force. You're using my momentum against me. I don't have any choice except to go where you take me. It doesn't matter how big or strong you are, or how big or strong I am. I'm going to teach you how to do this from every angle so no matter where someone is standing or how they try to grab you, you can use their momentum to put them on their butts."

That sounded good to Max.

IMPERFECT FIT

"I kind of think he sucks, too," Marina admitted to Max, quietly, like she was parting with an embarrassing secret.

Then she giggled.

They were talking about The Smoke. It was the longest conversation they'd ever had, and Max had to force himself to concentrate on the fact they were having it and stop listening to her so he could think about how awesome it was *that* they were having it.

He didn't know how he'd finally gotten over being too scared to talk to her. Maybe the note she'd slipped him after his "fight" with Johnny Pro helped. Maybe it was knowing Johnny Pro was gone for a while on the suspension they'd slapped him with after The Smoke's visit and all the internet attention. Master Plan had said it would take care of a bunch of their problems at once, and he'd been right as usual.

Whatever it was, their English teacher gave them a free reading period one day and Max turned to Marina and asked what she was going to read and, suddenly, they were talking.

They talked about their favorite characters in books, and that led them to talking about superheroes, and that led to talking about what a poseur they both thought The Smoke was.

Max really liked that she agreed with him about that.

"Either way," Marina said, "it's really great that he came here, right? I feel like that's why they finally punished Johnny."

She was smart, Max thought. No one else had figured that out besides him and Master Plan.

"Yeah, I guess. He'll be back, though."

Marina shook her head. "I don't know why he's so mean to you. You never did anything to him."

Max shrugged. "I make it easy, I guess. And the way I look doesn't help."

She frowned at him. "There's nothing wrong with the way you look."

"I don't even mean . . . It's not just being . . . big. I don't help it, I mean. I hate the clothes my mom buys me."

"Your shirts could . . . fit better," Marina admitted, obviously not wanting to hurt his feelings. "Not that anyone should mess with you because your shirt doesn't fit!"

Instead of feeling bad, Max actually smiled.

"No, you're right. That's what I mean about not helping myself."

"Maybe . . . like, have your dad help you shop? Maybe he'd understand more about buying clothes for a guy?"

"I don't really talk to my dad," Max explained without feeling one way or another about it. "My parents got divorced when I was a baby."

Marina looked at him differently than she had just a second before. She looked sad, but also kind of like what he just said made her feel better in some way.

"My dad . . . isn't around right now either," she told him.

"Oh. Can I ask what happened?"

"He just . . . he had to go away on business for a long time. Out of the country."

"Oh. I'm sorry."

"It's okay. My mom is great. She tries really hard."

"It can be tough, though," Max said. "With just one of them, trying to do everything. They're only one person, right? That's how I feel a lot of the time, anyway. Like I don't have as much of that . . . whatever . . . backup, I guess? As other kids?"

Marina nodded seriously. "That's totally it. It's just . . . it's really lonely sometimes, at home."

"Yeah."

She smiled at him then, and it wasn't the usual same kind smile she had for most everyone. It looked to Max to be more just for him, somehow.

It was one of the best feelings ever.

From: maximus928@gmail.com
To: 8mevojd@lightservice.net
Subject: Looking cool

How can I look better? I don't mean how can I be
skinnier. It's not about that. I just hate how I look. I hate
my hair. I hate my clothes. I see all these other kids,
like Johnny Pro. They have gel in their hair, or designs
shaved into it, or long hair like they are in a band even
though they are not. They all have their own style or
whatever. And it is like they just know how to do that.
Like somebody taught them.

No one ever taught me about that kind of stuff.
I feel like if I tried it would only make them come at
me harder. Like if I just show up at school one day
with my hair all combed or wearing a leather jacket or
something, they'd just make fun of me for that instead
of all the stuff they usually make fun of me for.

I feel like I'm stuck with how I am, even if I don't like
how I am.

My mom buys me these pants that are ugly colors.
There is this picture of me as a baby in red pants, and I
think she thought it was cute, because I feel like she has
bought me those pants in bigger sizes ever since.

Clothes never fit me, anyway. Clothes I like don't fit

me, I mean. I feel like anything cool is never in my size. For my birthday last year, my uncle gave me this shirt and hat, they were both Chicago Bulls. I don't even like sports, but he does. I don't know if he just didn't know any better, and he thought all boys my age like basketball or whatever.

I thought it would be cool to wear it anyway. Or like it would be better than the weak shirts I usually wear with nothing on them, or that come from some amusement park my mom took me to years ago. The shirt my uncle got me was way too tight. It made my stomach look even bigger, and it gave me boobs. My mom said maybe we could get the shirt in a bigger size, but they don't make one.

I didn't even want to wear it in the first place.

I know it's just a shirt, but I think about that a lot since it happened. All the clothes I wear feel like that day. I don't like looking in mirrors. I close my eyes a lot when I brush my teeth, or even when I brush my hair. If I'm wearing clothes or not, I always try to walk past them without seeing myself.

I just feel like if I could look better, like cooler or just more like not some chud, it would help with what we are trying to do at my school. And I might not hate looking at mirrors so much. That's all.

I'm sorry if this is dumb and I am wasting your time. Maybe it's not important. I just thought I would ask.

—Max

From: 8mevojd@lightservice.net
To: maximus928@gmail.com
Subject: RE: Looking cool

Maxwell,

Before we begin, never apologize to me, or to anyone else for
that matter, for speaking your truth. Never believe that what
you feel or what you want is "dumb," not to me or to yourself.
Denying our own feelings and desires keeps us from becoming
the people we want to be.

Appearance is a tricky thing. When adults tell you it doesn't
matter how you look, what they actually mean is it *should
not* matter how you look. And that is true. It shouldn't. The
others at your school shouldn't judge you or treat you badly
or differently because of how you dress, or how you wear your
hair. But they do, and they will. What is fair and what is right
isn't going to change that, unfortunately.

However, that does not mean *we* cannot bring about change
ourselves.

So then, let us speak about appearance, more specifically
yours. I understand why the incident with the shirt your uncle
gifted you has stuck with you so. It is these small things, one
after another after another, that when added up define who
we are. The "little things," as we think of them, are in truth
everything.

Those who make and sell clothing rarely think about people of size like us. You are correct when you write that you do not and should not need to be thinner to be happy with the way you look. You do not need to be thinner to change the way others view and treat you, either. Both of these things are much more about how you see yourself than the way others see you.

My advice is this: Do not change the way you look to make others happy. Change the way you look to make yourself happy. This is important for two reasons. The first is that people, even and especially others your age, can clearly see when you are doing something in order to try to impress or influence them. When that happens, they will only mock you for trying. The second reason is that doing things only to please others means you are never pleasing yourself. That is no way to live life.

If I may, I will use myself as an example for you. If I appear "cool" to you, it is only because you are seeing the confidence I have in myself, and in the way I look. I began wearing suits because when I first saw the way I looked in a suit it pleased me. That feeling gave me confidence. Once I started wearing them all the time, other people did not see a man in a nice suit. They did not treat me differently because I looked good in a suit. What they saw, what they responded to, was my confidence.

That is what is important. Choose clothes and hairstyles

and accessories that you like, that make you feel good about yourself. That feeling will show to others more than any of the specific items you choose or styling changes you make.

And whatever clothes you choose, some practical advice: Choose pants that fit. Larger bellies call for pants that fit over them instead of under them. You will feel more comfortable in them, and they will look better.

Also important: You should not try to change everything about the way you look all at once. If you turn up to school tomorrow looking totally different, your classmates will see it as a costume, both because of how shocking and sudden the change is, and because you won't look comfortable with the way you are yet.

Instead of trying to change your entire look all at the same time, start with just one thing. Choose a small thing. Give yourself time to get used to that little change. Give yourself time to feel comfortable with it. That will give you more confidence in how you look with this small difference, and then you can start adding to that.

My last piece of advice for introducing these changes in your appearance at school: Have a reason for the change you make. Have an explanation ready. In the beginning, and especially if any of your classmates accuses you of changing your appearance to try to influence how they see you, be able to give them a reason you had to make that change, something that made you do it that couldn't possibly have anything to do with you trying to "look cool."

Remember, my young friend, it is the small things. Begin there, and you can change everything.

Cordially,

Maximo

SEVEN DAYS TO A COOL NEW LOOK

DAY ONE

Max started with a new hoodie.

He'd never worn one before but had always wanted to. He always thought he had to be some kind of athlete to walk around in a hoodie because most of the kids who wore them at school seemed to be on a sports team, and their hoodies were all branded with the names of their teams.

Plus, he'd had an idea for the new look he wanted to try. His mom would never let him actually watch the show, but Max had seen commercials for a streaming series about outlaw motorcycle bikers, and the leader always wore a leather jacket over a hooded sweatshirt, with the hood handing down over the back of the jacket.

Max thought that looked tough.

For the past two years when the weather changed, he'd worn a big puffy winter jacket that Max thought made him look like a couch in the waiting room of a doctor's office.

Fortunately for Max, that coat had seen better days. It was being held together with more than a few drops of glue by the time it started getting cold enough outside to make him dig it out of his closet again. When his mom saw it, she decided to take him shopping over the weekend for new winter clothes.

Max had made the decision that no matter what else happened, he wasn't leaving the store with the same awful pants he'd been wearing to school his whole life. If he only managed to make one change, that was going to be it.

He didn't wear jeans because they had never fit him comfortably, but that was because the jeans his mom had bought for him in the past only fit him under his stomach. They slid down his hips when he walked unless he wore a tight belt, and the belt buckle always bit into the bottom of his stomach.

When he tried on a pair of jeans that fit around his stomach instead, like Master Plan had told him to get, it changed everything. Not only were they way more comfortable, but when he saw how they fit on him in the store mirror, Max thought they not only looked better, they actually looked good on him.

Even his mom was impressed, and not in that fake, automatic way moms are impressed with everything their kid does. She picked out three pairs to buy him, and Max told her he wanted to go check out the sportswear section.

The hoodie was black and dark gray, and when Max tried it on, he liked how it felt and how it looked. He thought the hoodie did for him what Master Plan's suits did for Maximo; they made his body look straight up and down instead of bulgy everywhere he didn't want it to be bulgy. Being inside of it made him feel safe and comforted. And the hoodie's dark colors and the way they were broken up with a straight line across the chest like a gunslinger's bullet belt made him think of one of his other favorite supervillains, Enigma.

Max knew a leather jacket wasn't happening—they were too expensive—but they found one that looked a lot like leather, with a thick and warm lining, and it had those worn-out spots that made it seem as though the jacket had been through a lot, even though it was brand-new. That reminded Max of how he felt most of the time.

His mom didn't argue or fuss with him about any of his choices. He wasn't sure why he expected her to, but he did. Max decided then it wasn't that she had been trying to dress him badly all these years, it was that she just didn't know any better, and he'd always simply gone along with whatever she bought him without giving his opinion on anything. It made him start thinking about a lot of other stuff he just let happen without saying anything.

The following Monday morning, he showed up to school in his same old dumb pants, but he wore his new hoodie. He kept his new jacket at home, knowing it wasn't time for it yet.

No one said anything about the hoodie. He was just another kid dressed for the changing weather. Max felt different, though. He didn't feel *a lot* different, but he felt a little spark, like the beginning of something good.

He also liked having the pockets in front to keep his hands. It stopped him from fidgeting so much, or feeling nervous. It helped him be more relaxed when he was sitting in class. And because he was wearing the hoodie, Max wasn't constantly pulling and tugging at and adjusting his shirt when he felt it riding up or bunching against him.

He didn't put up the hood, though. He wasn't ready for such a big move.

And Master Plan had told him to start small.

DAY TWO

Max wasn't sure he still had the ring.

His mom had bought it for him when she took Max

to a renaissance fair for his eleventh birthday. He saw the ring in one of the many booths selling all kinds of different crafts, from jewelry to real swords and axes. The ring was shaped like a roaring lion, and its whole body was the part that wrapped around your finger.

His birthday was in July, which made Leo his "star sign" (at least that's what his mother insisted; Max didn't really get what that whole thing was about). The symbol for Leo was the lion. His mom had even bought a big, shiny glass portrait of a lion to hang in their living room because of it.

Max had thought the ring was cool, but it was his mom who insisted they buy it. He had been too afraid to actually wear it, at least outside the house, and especially at school.

When he was in fourth grade, he'd really liked a show called *Ghostwriter*. It was about a bunch of kids who solved mysteries with the help of a ghost, who could only talk to them by moving the letters around in words that were written somewhere, whether it was in a book or on a sign or whatever. The kids talked back by writing the ghost notes, and they each carried pens that they wore on necklaces so they always had them close.

Max thought that awesome, and he liked to write, too. When he saw a pen like that at a drugstore, with a rubber cap on a necklace, he had to have it.

The very first day he'd worn it to school, an older boy had snatched the pen from its cap while Max was walking the hall at lunch. He'd flung the pen out a window, and he and his friends had laughed as Max ran to the window to try to spot where it had landed. He never did find it.

Max thought about that every time he even considered busting out his lion ring. It was a lot flashier than a pen on a string necklace.

He found the ring at the bottom of a drawer in the little desk in his bedroom.

He didn't wear it, but he started carrying it around in his pocket. It was going to be like the cherry on top of a sundae, and he hadn't finished making the sundae yet.

DAY THREE

In the morning, it started to rain, hard. Max was just leaving the house to walk to school when he felt the first drops, which quickly turned into a downpour.

At first he was just going to put up his hood and stuff his hands inside his pouch pockets and march through it, but then he had an idea.

Running back inside, Max went to his mom's bathroom and began digging through all the bottles of products under her sink. It took him a minute, but he found a squeeze bottle of hair gel that looked like it hadn't been used in years.

He pulled a comb out of a drawer and looked at himself in the mirror. Max had never put anything in his hair before other than shampoo, so he figured he'd start with a drop and then see if he needed more. It actually took enough drops to make up a handful of gel before he was able to comb all his hair straight back and have it stay that way.

When he was done, he thought he looked like Maximo without the beard. Master Plan had instructed Max not to copy him, but he also told him to make changes that made Max happy, and this one did. He thought it looked cool.

"Now, *who* is this and what have you done with *my* son?" his mom asked Max when he came out of the bathroom.

"What do you mean?" Max asked, as if he really didn't know.

She was smiling at him in a weird way Max couldn't quite figure out.

"What?"

"Is this about a girl?" she asked.

"Mom!"

Max ran out the door, mostly to escape having any

more of that conversation.

"You look handsome!" she called after him.

Later that morning, he sat in first period and peeled the wet hood back from his head, revealing his slicked-back hair. Max smoothed his ring finger over it, making sure it was flat and even.

A few kids gave him what he thought were strange looks, the kind you might get if you were missing your eyebrows, like something was different about your head but they couldn't decide what was off.

No one said anything to him, though.

It rained the next three days, and each morning Max slicked his hair back and showed up to class the same way. Eventually the rain had stopped, but Max was still wet and combed his hair straight back.

DAY FOUR

The scarf, pure white silk with a single dark red rose embroidered on one end of it, had belonged to his father.

Max hadn't told Master Plan anything about him yet, and Maximo had not asked.

The scarf was one of the only things of the man's that his mom had kept, actually. She said it was because it was an expensive accessory, but Max suspected she liked it because it reminded her of whatever it was she'd loved about Max's dad, not that he knew what that might be. She didn't talk about it much, if at all.

Max liked his father's scarf. He liked it a lot more than his father, in fact. It wasn't that Max hated the man. The truth was, when he thought about it, which wasn't often, Max didn't know his father well enough to like or dislike him. They never really spent enough time together for Max to form an opinion. He was just another person, like millions of others out there Max didn't know and would never know. It didn't change his life in the same way the rest of them didn't.

Sometimes that was worse for him than being mad at his father. Max wished he felt some way about it. Max pulled the scarf out of his mom's closet and hung it around his neck and then slid into his hoodie, zipping it up so that the scarf just barely peeked out. He thought it kind of made him like a boxer training for a big fight in an old movie.

There were plenty of kids at his school wearing scarves this time of year. He was just another one.

DAY FIVE

Max liked his language arts teacher, Ms. Franks. She was very kind, and he thought she really meant it. That was part of the reason he picked her.

They were having a free period during which she allowed the kids to read anything they wanted, as long as they read. It was also good because she let them all move desks or sit on the floor together in groups. It meant people were moving around a lot of the period.

Max waited until Ms. Franks left her desk for a minute, and when he was sure none of the others were paying attention, he took off his chunky black-framed glasses and placed them carefully on the seat of her chair.

He wandered away a little, pretending to read something on the board (which didn't make sense, seeing as how he'd just taken off his glasses, but no plan was perfect, he decided).

Less than a minute later, he heard the crunch, followed by Ms. Franks letting out a little yell. He hoped it was from surprised and not because she'd hurt herself.

"Omigod, Max! Are these yours?"

When he turned around, she was holding his glasses. She'd sat right down on them. They were practically snapped in half, and both lenses were cracked.

It was perfect.

"Yeah," he said.

"Why were they on the chair?"

"I just . . . I put them down for a second. I didn't think—"

"It's all right. I'm just sorry. Tell your mom I'll pay for new ones, okay? I feel really bad."

Max felt worse. But it had to be a teacher. His glasses had to break in a way where everyone would notice and remember, but it couldn't be another kid.

A few people laughed, and Max thought he even heard someone whisper "dork" about him, but Ms. Franks hadn't made a big enough deal about it that it stopped the whole class. A lot of people never even looked up from whatever they were reading.

He hadn't outright lied to his mom yet, about any of the things he'd done with Master Plan's advice. This time he had no choice. He told her his glasses had been broken "accidentally" and he needed new ones.

She fought him a little when they went to the store and he wanted new frames the same dark red color as the rose on his dad's scarf. His mom thought they were "too much," but he said he liked them and that those were the kind of frames kids who wore glasses at his school liked right now.

He didn't know if that was even close to true. He just knew *he* liked them, and thought they would look really dope matched to his dad's silk scarf.

When anyone in his classes asked what was up with the new glasses, Max just said his old ones broke and these were the only frames the store had. He got a couple of snickers from a few kids, but nobody decided to make a big thing out of it.

His reason seemed to satisfy everyone.

DAY SIX

One Monday not too long after that, the temperature outside dropped twenty degrees. Max wore his new jacket to school for the first time, over his gray-and-black hoodie, with the hood pulled out over the back of the jacket's collar just the way he'd imagined it in his head. He let his dad's scarf hang loose down the front so it could be seen, especially the rose, and he finally swapped out his hated red pants for the new jeans that actually fit him.

Max finished by giving his already-slicked hair a quick comb back and sliding on his ring and his new glasses.

"What's up with you?" Luca asked him at school later.

"What do you mean?" Max said, although he knew exactly what Luca meant.

In fact, he'd been afraid of that question. Luca was the one person who Max knew would notice the changes he was making.

"Your hair, the glasses, the clothes. Is this, like, a makeover?"

"No!"

"What, then?"

"I'm just . . . I'm trying some new stuff. I'm trying to not look like such a dork. Okay?"

Luca didn't say anything to that. He got this strange expression on his face, like Max had hurt his feelings or something.

Max hadn't expected that. He thought Luca might not understand or might make fun of him.

"What?" he asked his friend. "What did I do?"

"Nothing," Luca said quietly.

"What's wrong with you, then?"

"Nothing! I just . . . you look a lot cooler than me, I guess, that's all. And I can't . . ."

Max understood. Luca's mother and father had both been out of work for over a year. They couldn't afford to get him new clothes.

They'd always been friends partly because they were both the raggedy-looking kids in the class.

Max hadn't thought until that moment about what changing himself would do to their friendship.

He couldn't stop, though, not when he'd come so far already.

They didn't talk for the rest of the day.

DAY SEVEN

Two good things happened that day. The first was right before PE class. Max was rushing to his usual stall to change into his gym clothes when he accidentally caught sight of something he didn't usually like to look at: him.

This time he stopped to admire the sight, though. Max stood in front of one of the bathroom mirrors and stared for longer than he could ever remember looking at himself in a mirror before.

He liked what he saw. He looked like a different kid, but he still looked like him.

It was more like the picture of himself he had in his head than he ever remembered being before.

Max still went and changed inside the bathroom stall, but he felt different as he did, less bad about the whole situation than usual.

The second good thing happened before last period. It was the one class where Marina sat right behind him.

The bell had rung and they were all stuffing their books inside their backpacks, and suddenly Marina said to Max, "What's different with you?"

He looked up from zipping his bag. She was studying him like a math problem. Marina had never looked at him like that before and definitely not for that long.

"What do you mean?" he asked, trying not to sound like his heart was beating as fast as it absolutely was.

She shrugged.

"I dunno." Marina zipped up her own bag and shouldered it, not looking at him anymore as she said, "You look really cool, though."

She walked away from him, and when she was all the way gone, Max finally felt like he could breathe again.

You look really cool.

Max didn't know about that, but he *felt* cool.

From: maximus928@gmail.com
To: 8mevojd@lightservice.net
Subject: RE: Looking cool

It worked. It all worked.

I felt weird lying to my mom about my glasses. By "weird" I guess I mean I felt bad. I was thinking after that I could have just asked her for new glasses. But I needed a reason to change them, like you said, with the other kids in my class. And it worked. Marina said I look cool.

What's next?

—Max

From: 8mevojd@lightservice.net
To: maximus928@gmail.com
Subject: RE: Looking cool

Maxwell,

I am pleased to learn you are happier with and more confident in your appearance, and clearly your classmates are seeing that.

I value the truth greatly. That surprises many people. They think being a villain walks hand in hand with telling lies.

The truth, Max, is that we all lie, each of us, every day to everyone in a thousand different ways that are both spoken and unspoken; lies we mean to tell and don't mean to tell. Even the most honest of us do this, whether we can admit it to ourselves or not. We lie to other people in order to not hurt their feelings.

You have to choose how and why to lie. You did not lie to your mother in order to hurt her.

Now, to the business of what comes next for you and our mission.

One of the things that has kept you out of the groups formed by your classmates is that too many of them only think doing and being certain things are worthy. They do not believe you have the qualities they have been taught to think are the only qualities worth having. You are not an athlete. You are not a great speaker. It is okay to not be good at any of these things, and to not want to be good at them.

We have improved your look and, at least for now, we have removed your biggest threat to being accepted by having John Properzi sit out of school for a time. Next, we will help your other classmates see that what you have to offer as a person is worthy of their praise. You are good at many things. What we must do is teach your classmates to see value in what you do well, instead of looking down on it and you, because your skills do not match what they think of as valuable, or to put it another way, what they think is "cool."

To that end, I have arranged for an opportunity to present itself to you.

As I have told you before, I am only giving you advice. You must make the choice to act, and you must reach your goals on your own. You will have to decide to accept this opportunity, and if you do, you will have to make the most of it without my help.

I believe you will rise to the challenge, as you have done so far.

Cordially,
Maximo

OPPORTUNITY BAKED IN

"Yo, did you hear about that cooking thing?" Luca asked Max.

It was a perfectly ordinary sentence, even if Max didn't know what Luca was talking about. Something about the word "cooking" made Max's ears perk up, though.

They were in form class, the short fifteen-minute period they had at beginning of every day. Neither of them really understood what it was for yet. The teacher, Mr. Babich, didn't teach them anything. He mostly read his smart tablet, and sometimes he gave them announcements about school events or reminders about rules, usually if someone had broken one.

Things had been tense with Luca for a while after Max

remade his look, but a few days after that, they'd started talking again. Max still felt like there was some kind of weirdness between them, though. He didn't know how to talk to Luca about it.

"What cooking thing?"

Luca shrugged. "It's, like, a contest? A TV contest? I heard Mrs. Olivera talking about it this morning by the library. They're going to have the tryouts for it here. Like, at our school."

Max was even more confused now.

"Why would they do something for TV here?" he asked, although it wasn't really a question.

Luca only shrugged.

"Just thought I'd say 'cuz, y'know, you cook."

"No, I know, I'm just saying."

A few minutes later, Mr. Babich put his tablet down on his desk and looked up at them, although Max felt like he never really saw them.

"Hey, do any of you watch *Baked In*?" Mr. Babich asked.

Nobody said anything, which was normal. Kids in the class never seemed to answer a question unless it was to crack a joke.

Max knew better than to volunteer the information to the class that it was pretty much his favorite show on TV. Once he'd checked out three cookbooks from the library, each about food from different parts of the country. He was late returning them, and for some reason, they had his language arts teacher ask him about it in the middle of class, in front of everyone. When the other kids heard the title *Cooking in New England*, they laughed together at him for what felt like two straight minutes.

But *Baked In* was great. It was a weekly baking contest where four people were given mystery ingredients, and they had to bake it into different kinds of desserts, like cakes or brownies or pies. The secret ingredients got harder and often weirder in each round of the contest. One of Max's favorites was the episode where they gave the bakers popcorn and the winning contestant used melted butter and marshmallow to glue it into squares with raisins and chocolate so it was like mixing candy with your popcorn at the movies.

The desserts also had to look *good*. The way they were decorated was as much a part of how well they scored as the taste of each dessert. Max really liked decorating cakes and making plates of food that looked good, so it was one of his favorite parts.

"Anyway," Mr. Babich went on, "they're going to do a series of special episodes called *Baked In Junior*, for contestants between the ages of ten and thirteen. It's like a tournament, I guess. In order to pick all the kids who will be on the show, they're having little mini contests at schools all over the country, and they're going to film those, too. Our school has been picked to host one of these contests. Even though they're filming it here, it's going to be open to kids from all over the state. Principal Jones really wants one of our own kids to be in it, so if you want to know how to enter to be considered, come up and see me before the bell and I'll give you one of these handouts they sent us. There's also a website you can check out, and I'll just put the address up on the board. Okay?"

Again, nobody said anything, and most of the class returned their attention to their phones or whatever private conversation they were having before.

Mr. Babich also forgot about it pretty much as soon as he finished explaining the contest to them.

"Cool, good talk," he said to the class before putting his feet up on his desk.

"You should do it," Luca told Max, keeping his voice low so the other kids didn't hear. "You rule at all of that stuff, and we've watched every episode of that show. This is, like, *made* for you!"

I have arranged for an opportunity to present itself to you.

That's what Master Plan wrote to Max.

"Yeah, maybe," he said. "Maybe I should."

GLOB-UP

Max had a million ideas, all swirling and crashing into each other inside his head.

In order to be considered for the contest *Baked In* was filming at his school, he had to submit a video of one of his baking creations, an original recipe that he came up with and made all by himself. The handout Mr. Scott gave them from the show said that the creativity of the video itself would be part of how they picked the contestants and that they wanted kids with a lot of "personality."

The personality part worried him more than the baking part.

He knew people did "glow-up" videos online, where people changed themselves in some glamorous way, usually with makeup and new clothes. They edited the videos so the change looked like it happened in the blink of an eye. Max decided to make what he was calling in his head a "glob-up" video, transforming a boring-looking cake into a beautiful cake that he would make.

He started by getting everything ready in the kitchen. He put out all his ingredients. He plugged in the food processor. He got out mixing bowls, the whisk, and the spatula. Finally, he pulled from the cupboards all the pans he would need to bake the cake.

Max liked this part. Getting ready. Getting organized. It made him feel calm, and it shut his brain off. He didn't think about anything else except what was in front of him. He forgot about school and the other kids and what he didn't like about himself. That was one of the best parts about cooking for Max and why he liked it so much.

He didn't suppose it mattered that much how this cake tasted, since they were picking kids based on their videos, and not actually eating what they made. Still, Max decided to make his favorite batter for a cake, thinking he'd share it with his mom and save some for Luca.

His favorite kind of cake, at least for the spongy part before you frosted it, was banana cake. Max loved banana-flavored anything, really. He started the batter by mashing up some bananas they had that were starting to get brown. That was the secret. Older bananas with brown spots were softer and sweeter and made for better cake.

He put them in a bowl, and then in a separate bowl he mixed up flour, baking powder, baking soda, cinnamon, and a little salt. In a third bowl, he creamed together the butter and the sugar, hit it with a few drops of vanilla extract, and cracked two eggs into it before adding all the other stuff and some buttermilk and mixing everything together into a thick, soupy batter.

He poured half of the batter into one round cake pan, the inside of which he'd rubbed with oil to keep the cake from sticking when it baked, and the other half into another pan shaped just like the first. He'd started getting their oven hot before he arranged everything on the counter, so all he had to do was carefully slide both pans inside the oven and let them bake for forty-five minutes.

The whole time, his mom was recording short clips of him performing all the little baking tasks. They were going to edit them together before the big reveal in his audition video.

At one point, she lowered the phone she was using to record the videos while he was in the middle of getting things together to make the frosting.

Max became aware she was watching him instead of recording. She had a strange look on her face, kind of sad and happy all at the same time.

"What's wrong?" Max asked.

"You're really good at this," she said.

Max didn't really know what to say to that, so he just said, "Thanks."

"*Really* good, I mean," she repeated. "I know you can cook for yourself, but I just . . . I didn't really understand how *talented* you are."

His cheeks flushed red.

"Mom, stop."

"No, it's important," she insisted. "I feel like I miss way too much around here, working so much. I should've noticed. And told you."

"It's okay, Mom. You do what you have to do. For us. I get that."

She smiled at him. Max thought she was going to cry.

"You're a pretty smart kid," she said, swallowing back the tears before they could get away from her.

"Can we finish the video, please?" he asked, because he didn't want to talk about this anymore.

It had felt good to hear her say that about him, though. It occurred to Max he always thought of his baking as something to hide from other kids so they didn't make fun of him, not something he should feel proud about. No one besides Luca had ever really made a big deal about it before or told him how talented he was. Even Master Plan, who encouraged Max, talked about it more like something they had to figure out how to use in their plans.

His mother nodded. "Yes! Let's do this! Keep going!"

She raised the phone, and even though it'd made Max happy to hear what she said, he was glad to have the phone separating them again.

Making cake frosting was easy enough. It was mostly just butter and powdered sugar mixed together. You could add other things to give it different flavors, and food coloring or fruit to make it different colors.

He wasn't sure why, but Max started thinking about Marina. He tried not to watch her when she wasn't looking, because he knew that was creepy, but he couldn't help noticing things, like the colors of the clothes she seemed to like to wear best. They were always bright and reminded him of summer, a lot of yellows and reds and dark oranges, like fire.

He couldn't decide which of the three colors to make the frosting, and then it hit Max. He would make the cake all three colors at the same time, not by making one frosting that was all the colors mixed together, but by making three different frostings, a red one, a yellow one, and a dark orange one.

Even though they were all going to be different colors,

they would all be the same flavor so it wouldn't taste weird when he mixed them together. Max put butter and powdered sugar in the food processor, adding cream cheese because it went good with the banana cake, and locked the lid on before blending it all together. The food processor lid had a small opening on top of it, and after a few seconds, Max poured some yellow food coloring through it into the frosting mixture. A few seconds after that, the whole thing was a bright yellow.

Max did the same thing two more times with the other colors until he had small bowls of each kind of frosting. By then he only had to wait a few minutes for the cakes to be done baking. He knew they were done by sticking a toothpick into the top of each one, and when it came out clean, that meant the sponges were ready.

He let the sponge of his cake cool, and after frosting each layer Max stacked one cake on top of the other and began spreading frosting on the whole thing, one color at a time. After he'd covered the cake, he ran the straight edge of his metal spatula around the whole thing to make the frosting smooth and even. Doing that also blended the three colors into one thing.

What he ended up with reminded Max of a morning sunrise, and he thought it looked beautiful. The sunrise part also gave him another idea.

He looked up a video on how to make lollipops. He'd

never made candy before, let alone something that seemed as complicated as sugar glass. The thought of trying it for the first time for something as important as this made him nervous, but he knew Master Plan would've told him to go for it and trust himself to be able to pull it off.

Max poured sugar, water, and corn syrup into a small saucepan and heated it on the stove, slowly. The video said if he got it too hot too fast it would stick together and to the pan. He also needed to stir it until it got to be between 290 and 300 degrees Fahrenheit. Max felt himself sweat from the top of his head as he kept the mixture moving inside the saucepan. It wasn't from the heat; he was just sure he was going to screw this up somehow.

His mom had bought him a cool cooking thermometer for his birthday that told you how hot food was just by you pointing the thermometer at it, like a gun. He used it to check the temperature of the sugar glass, and when he pointed the thermometer at the top of the mixture, the little screen on it read *294°F.*

Now that it was hot enough, Max added yellow food coloring and stirred it in. He got a baking sheet ready by lining it with a silicone pad that wouldn't stick to the hot sugar glass. Max carefully began pouring the mixture from the saucepan onto the middle of the silicone, dribbling it very slowly and letting it spread into a circle. When the circle was the size Max wanted, he stopped pouring.

All he could do then was wait for the sugar glass to cool and harden. If the circle cracked or broke apart, he would have to start all over again.

It took almost two hours. Max started to freak out after a while. His mom made him go watch Netflix to take his mind off it. He watched an old episode of *Baked In*, the one where they gave the contestants raw hamburger and mushrooms as the secret ingredients, and honestly it just made him even more nervous.

"Max, I think it's ready!" his mom finally called to him from the kitchen.

He ran faster than he had in PE class all year. The big yellow sugar glass circle looked shiny and hard, like a colored windowpane.

Max picked up his spatula and very, very gently tapped the sugar glass with the end of the tool.

It didn't break, but it wasn't soft or soggy either.

It was perfect. He'd nailed it on his first try.

Feeling more confident, Max made another batch, but this time he dyed the sugar glass mixture orange, and when he poured it out onto the silicone, he made two circles, both the same size, both smaller than the first one he'd formed.

When everything was cool and hardened and ready, he carefully poked the bottom edge of the big yellow lollipop into the top of the cake, right in middle. Once he was sure it would stand up by itself, he let go of it and did the same thing with the smaller, orange lollipops, standing one up on each side the big yellow one.

It looked *sick*. The candy circles matched the frosting perfectly, and made the whole cake look even more impressive.

Max finished off his audition cake by piping some more frosting in little decorative twists around the edges of the top and bottom of the cake, and then he declared it was done.

He and his mom both stepped back to take in the finished product. Max looked up at her, and he thought she was about to cry again.

"It's beautiful, honeybun."

He'd always hated that nickname, but somehow after the talk they'd had before he made the frosting, Max didn't mind it so much in that moment.

And he agreed with her about the cake.

"I've never seen you work that long or that hard on anything," his mom said, sounding even more impressed than before.

"Just trying to make the most of an opportunity," he told her, staring at his creation with pride.

"So are we ready to do the video part?"

Max nodded, taking a long, deep breath. He felt tired, but he wanted to finish the project.

For the opening shot of the video, he wore his old clothes. He had his mom get him a packaged cake with plain white frosting from the store that was the same size as the one Max had baked. She thought it was a great idea and helped him record everything with her phone.

Once they got a shot of him standing in front of the boring cake, she stopped videoing and he went into his room and changed into his new clothes, slicking his hair back with gel in the bathroom and changing his broken glasses for his new ones.

When he got back to the kitchen, his mom had already replaced the plain cake with his sunrise one. Max stood behind it, smiling, and spread out his arms like he was presenting it to the camera.

It would look like both he and the cake had transformed instantly right before the contest judge's eyes when the two shots were edited together.

He didn't know if it would work, but he was proud of the cake he'd baked, and he was proud of the video when it was done.

And when they finally got to have a piece, both his mom, and Luca the next time he came over, told him the banana cake was delicious.

Max only wished he could've sent a slice to Master Plan.

ADVANTAGES

Luca was waiting for him on the steps in front of Max's front door. The sun was setting, and it was going to be dark soon. Usually Luca had to go home by then.

His mom had just driven them home from Max's latest class with Gunnar. Max was feeling good until he spotted Luca, and then a sinking feeling upset his stomach. Somehow he knew his friend wasn't going to be glad to see him.

"What are you doing sitting outside like this so late, Luca?" Max's mom asked, concerned, after they'd gotten out of the car and walked over to the steps.

"Uh. Waiting, I guess."

"Well, I don't want your mom to get worried. Isn't she expecting you at home?"

"Yeah, probably."

"Okay, well, you two say good night and then you head home, okay? Do you need a ride?"

"No, thank you, I'm okay."

Max's mom went inside, leaving them by themselves at the bottom of the steps.

"Where have you been, man?" Luca asked him. "You disappeared after last bell, and I knocked like five times."

"I was, uh, at class."

"What, that karate class? Again?"

Max bit his lip. He'd told Luca his mom put Max in "karate" after school because he didn't want to have to explain what Systema was, or how he'd found out about it.

"I thought that was just like once a week?"

Max shrugged. "I started going a few more times a week. So what?"

"You didn't tell me that!"

"You didn't ask!"

"I shouldn't have to!"

"Why are you mad?"

"Because!"

"Because why?"

Luca didn't say anything. Max wasn't sure whether he was being quiet because he didn't know what to say, or because Luca couldn't make himself say whatever he was thinking.

"You could take the classes with me, you know," Max said quietly, trying to make things better between them somehow.

That just made Luca more upset, though.

"You know my mom and dad can't pay for that!"

Max frowned. Not because of Luca, but because Max knew he shouldn't have said that. He should've known better.

"Well . . . I could teach you some of what I've been learning," Max offered.

Luca seemed to perk up at that.

"Really?"

Max nodded enthusiastically

"Sure!"

Max stepped in front of his friend and his body took the fighting stance Gunnar had taught him almost on its own. The stances and movements were starting to feel natural to Max, like walking or breathing. The more you did it, the more your body and brain worked together like a machine. You barely had to think.

"Okay, so, stand like me," Max told Luca. "You want your feet to kind of line up with your shoulders, and bend your knees just a little."

Luca did as Max instructed, trying to mirror his friend. He looked awkward doing it, like he had rocks in his shoes or something.

"Just relax," Max said.

"I am!" Luca insisted, snapping at him a little.

Max didn't think he was really mad. Luca just didn't want to look foolish in front of him, Max figured.

"Okay, that's good," he told Luca, even though his stance wasn't that good. "So it all starts with teaching your body to be aware, so that, like, the second you feel something touch you, your body is trained to move away from it before it can hurt you."

"What do you mean?" Luca asked, clearly confused.

In answer, Max reached out and poked him in the shoulder with two fingers, probably harder than he meant.

"Ow!" Luca reached up and rubbed the offended spot. "Jerk!"

"So yeah, when you feel me touch you, turn your body away from where my fingers are hitting."

"Say that first next time, then!"

"Sorry."

Max was starting to think this was a bad idea. He wasn't an instructor like Gunnar. But he also wanted to make Luca feel less like Max wasn't including him.

"Tell you what," he said. "Let me show you. Try to push me with your hand."

"Where?"

"Wherever."

Luca nodded. He bent his knees again, readying himself, and flung his hand out at Max's right shoulder.

Max turned at the waist before Luca's arm was even halfway extended toward him, and by the time Luca's hand reached Max, his shoulder wasn't there anymore.

Luca blinked and then immediately tried shoving Max's other shoulder.

Again, Max moved away from his hand before Luca could even graze him.

"Dude, when did you get so fast?" Luca demanded, sounding more annoyed than impressed.

Max shrugged. "You just do it over and over again, and it happens all by itself, almost. Try again."

Luca did, this time trying to shove Max right in the middle of his chest with both hands.

Max didn't even move his feet. He simply sucked in his gut and bent at the waist, out of Luca's reach.

Clearly frustrated, Luca stepped forward and shot his right arm out, almost like he was going to punch Max instead of push him. Max avoided the blow easily, confused as he watched Luca get angrier and angrier every time he tried to touch Max and missed.

After half a dozen more unsuccessful tries, Luca finally lost it. He yelled out like some kind of Viking on TV, charging at Max full speed like he was going to tackle him.

Max didn't have time to think. The training he'd been doing with Gunnar took over. When Luca reached out for him, Max stepped to one side, his leg sweeping Luca's ankles out from underneath him.

It was almost like slow motion, as Max watched Luca fall onto the sidewalk. Max winced as if he were the one hitting the ground.

"*What* was *that*, man?" Luca practically spat at him, stumbling back to his feet. "What're you *doing*?"

Max took a step forward, wanting to help him, but Luca backed away.

"Just forget it!" Luca said bitterly. "Never mind! I'm going home!"

"Dude, I'm sorry."

"Forget it, I said!"

Luca turned and had already stormed halfway up the block by the time Max could even start to think of what else to say.

He watched his friend walk away from him. Max was breathing hard, even though he didn't feel like he'd moved around that much. He felt confused, nervous, sad, and excited all at the same time. He didn't want Luca to be mad at him, and Max really hadn't meant to hurt him or put him down like that.

But he also couldn't help being happy that Gunnar's training had worked *so well*.

CHANGING

The other fat kid's name was Adolfo. He was the one Max had been racing to the bathroom stall in the locker room to change before PE class since school began.

Max finally learned his name one day when he decided to end their unspoken competition for the stall. He hadn't planned to do it. He hadn't even been thinking about it. Max just found himself in front of the stall door in the locker room one day, and as he reached for the handle something stopped him. He started thinking, asking himself if he was doing this because he was still scared, or because he'd just gotten used to it.

He heard his fellow fat kid shuffling up behind him a moment later, and Max turned away from the stall door to face him. The larger boy's sweater-vest of the day was black and fuzzy. Max decided it looked good on him. He finally understood why the other boy wore them all the time.

"Hey," Max said to him.

The boy blinked really fast without answering at first.

"Uh, hey," he finally said.

"I'm Max."

"Um. I'm Adolfo."

Max could see Adolfo was nervous and anxious about getting inside the stall to change, the same way Max had felt every day before PE class.

That was before, though. Max didn't feel anxious in that moment. He felt okay about not getting the stall to himself before class.

"It's all yours, Adolfo," Max said.

He hoped he didn't sound like he thought he was better than the other boy. That wasn't how Max meant it.

Adolfo still looked confused, but he didn't have time to question Max, and he was more than happy to take advantage of whatever weird mood Max seemed to be in that day.

After Adolfo had locked himself inside the stall, Max walked over to the nearest open locker. There were a few other sixth graders huddled together a few lockers down, talking about something Max wasn't paying close enough attention to hear. They didn't seem to even notice him.

Max started by carefully removing and folding his prized jacket and hoodie and stacking them gently inside the locker. He changed out of the rest of his clothes quickly, but made himself not hurry too much, or at least he hoped it didn't look like he was trying to hurry.

He didn't look up the whole time, so he couldn't be sure, but Max didn't feel any of the other boys watching him. He didn't hear anyone making fun of him.

And so what if they did, anyway? he thought. *Who cares what they think?*

Once he was changed into his uncomfortable gym clothes—feeling less scared and weird about his body around other kids didn't make the clothes fit any better—and he'd locked up his other things, Max glanced over at the closed door of his old bathroom stall.

He felt bad for Adolfo, too. Max thought now that they knew each other's name and weren't locked in a silent battle over the right to the safety of that stall, maybe he could ask if Adolfo wanted to change next to him out by the lockers. There was strength in numbers, and in having friends around you when you did things that were scary.

Max wondered if Master Plan would agree with that. Maximo always did everything on his own, after all. He didn't have "friends." He had henchmen.

Max had never written anything about PE class to

Master Plan. Maybe it was the one thing he was too embarrassed to admit to Maximo, he thought.

In any case, it wasn't something he needed Master Plan's help with anymore. Max realized he'd taken care of this on his own. Everything Master Plan had helped him do up to now made it easier, sure, but this was the first problem he'd had with sixth grade that he didn't need Maximo's advice to solve. That felt good, but also a little strange. He almost felt guilty, like not including Master Plan in this was somehow betraying him.

DON'T CALL IT A COMEBACK

Max was starting to forget what it felt like to show up for school in the morning afraid.

He was nervous that morning, but it had nothing to do with school. He was thinking about whether or not he'd get a chance to compete for a spot on *Baked In Junior*. He hoped the video his mom helped him make would be enough. Master Plan had told him it was an opportunity, and that Max would have to take advantage of it. If he'd learned one thing about his new friend, it was that Master Plan always meant what he wrote.

Max didn't know when he'd started thinking of Maximo Marconius as his friend. He wondered if that was just him wishing for something that hadn't happened yet, but he couldn't think of another word for someone who'd done as much to help him as Master Plan had without any reason to do so. Max had supposed maybe he was just bored, but he didn't think someone as smart as Master Plan really ever got bored.

He walked across the quad on his own, not sure where Luca was that morning and still feeling like that was probably for the best right now. He wasn't sure what to say to his only *other* friend.

Over the past few weeks, Max had stopped fearing the sight of school team jackets. He'd gotten use to passing them in the halls without anything bad happening. They'd started to become just part of the background of his everyday life, instead of a warning flag for him to run and hide.

That might be why he didn't notice John Properzi until he became a roadblock stopping Max from taking another step.

Johnny Pro seemed even taller than he had the last time Max had stood next to him. He was staring down at Max with his lips pressed tight and his eyes almost burning.

"Coach told me if I ever want back on the team that I better not even talk to you," he told Max, practically shaking with anger. "But I'm gonna tell you one thing right now. This isn't over. I can't do anything to you here at school. But the first time I see you off campus, especially with no parents or teachers around, you're dead meat. You think a couple punches hurt? You don't even know what 'hurt' means. I want you to know what's coming."

Max couldn't feel his own tongue. He was worried he'd swallowed it down into his throat.

He also barely noticed that as soon as he recognized Johnny Pro his body had shifted itself into the stance Gunnar had taught him.

"And your hair looks like a dog peed on your head," Johnny Pro informed him.

He walked away from Max without another word, and without laying a finger on him.

It took a minute for Max to start breathing regularly again. He looked around the quad. A few kids glanced back, but nobody really seemed to be paying attention to what just happened between him and Johnny Pro. Everything was quiet. Everyone was just going on with their mornings.

That made him calm for some reason. That calm helped Max realize something else. He wasn't scared. He'd been surprised to run right into Johnny Pro like that, maybe even shocked. That surprise had frozen him for a minute.

Now that Johnny Pro was gone, though, Max wasn't

shaking. His stomach wasn't knotted up or bubbling. His legs didn't feel weak. He didn't feel tears threatening to spill from his eyes. It wasn't like all the times before after Johnny Pro had walked away from Max.

Part of him felt relief knowing Johnny Pro couldn't mess with him at school anymore. But there was another part of Max that was almost disappointed. He wasn't the same terrified sixth grader Johnny Pro had been suspended for beating up. He didn't look the same, and he didn't feel the same anymore. Maybe it was training with Gunnar. Maybe it was all the advice Master Plan had given him, and everything Maximo had taught him. Maybe it was Marina treating him like he was cool. Maybe it was all those things.

Max had written to Master Plan that he just wanted Johnny Pro and every kid like him to leave Max alone. He wasn't sure that was true anymore. He wasn't sure that was good enough, not after everything Johnny Pro had done to him, and everything Max had to do to get him to stop.

Max wanted more than Johnny Pro to get a suspension and not get to play a dumb sport anymore. That wasn't punishment, not really.

He couldn't go after Johnny Pro, though. Master Plan would never be okay with him doing that. Max didn't even know *how* he would go about it.

But if Johnny Pro ever did get the chance to come at Max, that wouldn't be his fault.

If that happened, Max decided he'd get some *real* revenge.

From: maximus928@gmail.com
To: 8mevojd@lightservice.net
Subject: Baked In

I found out today that I'm going to be one of the kids who will compete at my school to be on *Baked In Junior.*

I know you got them to record the tryouts at my school. I don't know how, but I figure somebody who once stole an entire skyscraper can figure out how to do anything.

You said I would have to do this myself. I believed you. But I still just need to know, did they pick me because of my video? Did they pick me because of what I did? Or did you make that happen, too?

I guess it doesn't matter. Except it kind of does matter to me.

You keep saying that you are just giving me advice. I guess I just want to know that is still true, and that I did this myself.

You were right, my new clothes and my new hair and everything help give me confidence, but they are not enough. I feel like I need to be able to do more than look different if I want to feel different. Maybe if I can do good in this contest that will be the something else I need.

Does that make sense?

—Max

COMPETITION

They called an all-school assembly after second period, and no one Max overheard talking knew what it was about.

"It's about you, dummy," Luca told him.

"Huh?"

"You got that email about being picked for the baking contest. They're going to tell the whole school and probably call you up onstage."

Max's eyes grew wide.

"Nobody said anything about that!"

"You heard Mr. Babich say that Principal Jones really wanted a kid from this school to be in the contest. Of course he's going to make a big deal about it."

Max hadn't told anyone except Luca about the email, or about getting into the on-screen tryouts. He hadn't even wanted to tell Luca, but he needed something to talk to him about after their fight on the sidewalk. It was big enough news that it got Luca over what had happened between them. Max wasn't sure why he'd wanted to keep the news a secret, or what he expected to happen. The whole point of doing this was supposed to be that everyone at his school would know about it. Max just didn't want to be the one to tell them.

He supposed if Luca was right he was about to get his wish.

Luca shook his head, but he was also grinning. "You are the dumbest smart kid I know sometimes, man. How did you not figure this out?"

"Shut up," Max grumbled.

"It really was a good cake."

"Shut up," Max repeated, and then added quickly, "Thanks, though."

A few minutes later, Principal Jones took to the stage in front of all his students. He always reminded Max of Nick Fury from the Marvel movies, only without the patch over one eye. Max was scared of him but liked him at the same time.

There was a single microphone set up at the front of

the auditorium stage, and Principal Jones stepped in front of it, looking comfortable and confident in his suit and tie in a way that reminded Max of Master Plan.

"As you all know, in a couple of weeks we have the honor of hosting a film crew, as well as the star judges and host of the television program *Baked In*. Four lucky young people from our home state will be competing right here on this stage. The winner will go on to compete against young bakers from all over the country as part of the program's special *Baked In Junior* tournament, which will air over several weeks on the Kitchen Channel."

There was a small chorus of cheers and applause, but most the kids in the audience remained silent.

"It's a very exciting event," Principal Jones said, less like he was excited about it and more like he was telling them *they* should be *more* excited about it. "What makes it even more exciting, however, is the following announcement, and the reason we've called this assembly today. I am so very proud and pleased to announce that out of the hundreds of young bakers who submitted videos, *two* of the *four* kids chosen from our area to compete for a chance to be on *Baked In Junior* are students *right here* at Captain Clobbertime Memorial Middle School!"

Max's head whipped to look at Luca, who stared back with the same surprise on his face. *That* announcement got everyone's attention.

"Two?" Max asked.

"It's not me," Luca assured him.

Max looked around to see dozens and dozens of seventh and eighth graders sit up in their chairs. It seemed like everyone who wasn't interested only a second ago was now listening very intently to what their principal was saying.

"Ladies and gentlemen and all of our nonbinary students . . . let's give a big round of applause for the two young bakers who will represent our school, both from our sixth-grade class, Maxwell Tercero and Marina Martine!"

Max didn't hear his classmates cheering around him, three times as loud as they had before. He was too shocked to hear anything in that moment.

Marina?

"Come on up here, Marina and Maxwell!" the principal instructed them from the stage.

Max heard that. There was no doubt about it.

She was sitting a few rows in front of him, and Max watched as Marina and her friends freaked out in their seats, screeching and laughing. Marina had her hands cupped over her mouth. Her eyes were big and sparkling green. The other girls excitedly shoved her out of her chair and into the aisle, and soon Marina was half running, half skipping up to the stage to join Principal Jones.

"Go on, dude, get up there!" Luca hissed in his ear. "He called your name, too!"

Max nodded dumbly, feeling himself lift out of his chair, even though he didn't feel like he was telling his legs what to do. It was more like he floated up to the stage than walked. Everything looked and felt and sounded very weird, like a dream.

He stood on one side of Principal Jones and Marina stood on the other side. It helped a little not to be able to see her. He was almost able to catch his breath.

Max blinked out over the hundreds of his classmates, all of them watching him. No one booed. No one yelled out insults. No one called him fat. It wasn't like the time in language arts class when the teacher asked if he'd checked out all those cookbooks from the library.

"Folks, let's hear it for your classmates Marina and Max! I know they're going to rep this school to the best of their abilities!"

Everyone clapped, and this time it sounded louder and more like they were all doing it because they were excited, and not just because they were supposed to clap.

For just a second, Max forgot that Marina's name had been called alongside his. He smiled a slow, nervous smile, his stomach doing flips as he watched the whole school cheer for him.

It lasted for another minute, and then Principal Jones called an end to the assembly. He shook Max's hand and congratulated him, told him he would be calling his mom to talk about filming the tryouts at the school.

Max walked offstage. He had to walk slowly, because he was worried if he tried to move too fast he would fall over. It was all too much. He had to remind himself to breathe like normal.

Someone grabbed on to his arm, hard, and he flinched, like Johnny Pro and his squad was about to start whaling on him.

It was only Marina, though. She'd ran up to him, smiling from ear to ear, looking flushed and out of breath.

"Omigod, Max! I didn't know you liked to bake, too!"

She didn't look or sound mad, or like she was worried about competing against him. Seeing that made Max feel a little better.

"Do you cook, too?" Marina asked him, still excited.

Max managed to nod.

"What do you cook?"

"Um, all kinds of stuff. My grandma taught me how to do, like, Southern food, mostly? Like fried chicken, and she made really good beans with hamburger. And she taught me how to bake a few things. That's how I started baking."

"My grandmother taught me, too! My mom's mom! Is your grandma still around?"

Max shook his head.

The look on Marina's face got more serious.

"Mine either," she said. "It sucks, doesn't it?"

"I didn't feel good for a long time after," Max admitted, and he couldn't remember ever saying that to anyone, even his mom.

Marina nodded, but then she brightened a little.

"I wish I'd known a long time ago you were into cooking and baking! We could have been talking about recipes and stuff for, like, the whole year already!"

Max wondered suddenly if that was true. He wondered if he'd gotten up the guts to talk to Marina about cooking back when Johnny Pro was beating him up every day, would she have been this excited?

"Can I see your audition video and what you made?" Marina asked. "I'll show you mine?"

"Yeah, sure."

Marina took out her phone, and suddenly they were huddled together, watching their videos and talking about their recipes and how they'd put everything together.

Max didn't remember much of what they said to each other later, he only remembered how he felt talking to her so close and for so long.

It was a feeling he definitely wanted more of.

From: 8mevojd@lightservice.net
To: maximus928@gmail.com
Subject: RE: Baked In

Maxwell,

First, congratulations on seizing the opportunity that presented itself to you.

Second, let us speak of cheating and of advantages, because they are very different things.

This television program coming to your school wouldn't have happened without some maneuvering on my part, it is true. But I did not help you with your audition video, and I did not influence the judges on your behalf. I gave you an advantage. You took that advantage and made the most of it. This is not the same thing as cheating.

Be proud of yourself. Feel confident in yourself. You did this on your own, and what happens next is also up to you.

Marina being in the contest is also an advantage, although I am sure the surprise of it made that hard to see for you at first. However, this will be an experience you can share with her that will bring you closer. It does not matter whether you win or lose, or whether she wins or loses. You are representing your fellow classmates, who now see the value in you and your culinary talent. There is nothing more highly prized in our culture than being on television.

In short, they think you are cool now.

That is all we were trying to make happen. And it has.

Do your best in the competition and make a good showing, and I assure you they will all treat you very differently from now on.

Cordially,

Maximo

PIECE OF CAKE

Max had never felt more nervous in his entire life. He just wanted to bail. He wanted to run out of the auditorium and hide in the back seat of his mom's car. There was no way he could do this. He'd never done *anything* in front of a group of people this big.

The only thing that kept him from running out of the auditorium was thinking about having to write to Master Plan to explain that he quit. Max couldn't do that.

All he had to do was put on a good show. He didn't even have to win. He kept reminding himself about that.

He was standing just offstage, in a group with the other three kids who were competing in the tryouts. There was Marina, a seventh grader from upstate who was even larger than Max and wearing a bow tie (he had more courage than Max, with or without the help of a master supervillain, and Max admired him for it), and a very tall eighth-grade girl with braces.

They were all nice. Max wondered why cooking and baking seemed to make kids nicer. He wished they'd teach a class on it at his school. Maybe he wouldn't even need Master Plan's help if they did.

His mother and Luca were both in the front row, out in the audience. The auditorium was packed. It looked like the whole school *and* their parents.

From what the producer said to them, they weren't going to show the whole contest here today on *Baked In*. They were just going to show little clips of how each winner made it onto *Baked In Junior*.

The three judges from the actual show were there, though. Max recognized them from TV. They were going all around the country to the different mini contests to judge them and pick the kids for the *Baked In Junior* tournament.

There was Bronko Luck, a famous chef on television who had a bunch of different shows of his own over the years. He was a giant of man who looked more like a football linebacker than a cook. He was always the nicest one out of all the judges to the contestants.

The second judge was Aunt Lexi, a world-class baker who had a chain of cookie shops named after her, the ones you always saw at the mall. She was the toughest on the bakers and their desserts, but Max thought she was fair.

The final judge was Zero Effect, an old superhero who retired from crime fighting when Max was in kindergarten. He used to be able to move objects as large as a dump truck by pointing his finger at them, but ever since The Aggressor dropped him on his head from a hundred-foot building, Zero Effect couldn't move anything bigger than a saltshaker. Sometimes he would move bites of food into his mouth using his powers, but Max always thought he looked nervous when he did it.

It seemed to Max that whenever a superhero couldn't "fight crime" anymore, they ended up judging reality-TV-show contests.

And then there was the host of the show, who did most of the talking and interviewed the bakers. His name was Bones Gormley. Max didn't much like him. He had a face like a hairless weasel and he liked to make fun of the contestants, and they always had to laugh at his dumb jokes. He reminded Max a lot of Johnny Pro, actually.

In addition to a whole bunch of people with cameras and sound equipment, the crew from the show had transformed the stage of their auditorium into a kitchen. There were four ovens with stoves and four tables, and one station for each of the kids competing. They'd set up a pantry and a bunch of refrigerators in the back of the stage with all kinds of baking equipment and ingredients, stuff Max had never seen before.

He waited with the others, trying hard not to throw up, but also almost wanting to throw up just so he could feel better afterward.

"Are you nervous?" Marina asked him.

"Nah," Max said, trying to sound like he meant it.

"Really?"

Max laughed nervously.

"I'm so freaking scared."

Marina grinned. "Me too."

He felt something and looked down.

Marina was squeezing his hand.

A blond woman wearing a headset and carrying a clipboard walked over to them and said, "All right, kids, are you ready?"

She didn't wait for any of them to answer before continuing with "Bones—you all know Bones—he's going to get us started in a second, and he'll bring you all out. You've been given your numbers. When you walk out onstage, just go to the station with your number. That's where your oven and worktable and everything is. Easy, right?"

Max wondered if she'd still say that if she were the one about to bake something from scratch with a secret ingredient in front of their whole school.

He didn't say that, though.

Eventually Bones Gormley stepped to the middle of the stage with a microphone and greeted the cheering crowd. Bones introduced each of the judges, who stood and waved, and the crowd cheered even louder for them.

"Now, let's meet our potential junior bakers!"

He meant them.

Max didn't move at first. In fact, Marina had to pull him along by the hand just to get his feet going. He watched their hands joined together as they walked out onto the stage, and then Marina let go of him.

The audience cheered the loudest for the four of them that they cheered yet. Two weeks ago, he'd never heard anyone clapping and hollering for him, let alone a room full of hundreds of people, and a lot of them the same kids he used to be afraid to come to school with every day.

Max had the third station. He stood next to his worktable and tried to look at the crowd without actually seeing them. It helped keep his stomach calm.

Bones Gormley was handed a tray with a cloth covering something on it.

"All right, as you all know from watching the show, we

185

can't get started until you have your secret ingredient! Is everyone ready to find out what it is?"

The crowd cheered their approval.

"Your secret ingredient today is . . ."

Bones Gormley whipped the cloth away from the tray with a flourish.

"Jalapeño peppers!"

Everyone gasped.

Bones wasn't kidding. There were six big green peppers arranged on top of the tray.

Peppers? What am I supposed to do with peppers? Peppers don't go in desserts, right? I've never put peppers in something sweet. . . .

Max's brain could've gone on like that forever, but Bones Gormley was saying more words, and he knew he should probably listen.

"Okay! The four of you will have two hours to come up with and bake a sweet dessert of your own creation that uses these peppers in some major way. Your bake will be judged on taste, presentation, and how you incorporate our secret ingredient. Are you ready?"

Max definitely wasn't, but he knew saying that wouldn't help or change the situation.

"Is our audience ready?!" Bones asked the crowd.

They not only cheered, a bunch of them started chanting the name "Marina."

And, to his surprise, a bunch of other kids started chanting, "Max! Max! Max!"

That should probably have made him feel good, he supposed, but it actually made him even more nervous.

"All right!" Bones Gormley announced to the four of them. "Your two hours starts right now! Good luck!"

Max knew he had to block out everything. He had to forget about the crowd. He had to forget about the judges. He had to forget about the other contestants, including Marina, who were all running around gathering ingredients and equipment like they knew exactly what they were going to do.

He had to make all of it disappear from his sight and his mind and just focus on the problem of deciding what to bake.

Except Max had nothing. He couldn't think of a single idea. He couldn't even remember recipes he knew, let alone come up with a new one. He tried to recall how to make a simple batter, for *anything*. It was like he'd forgotten everything he ever knew about baking.

What was he going to do? How did you disguise a hot pepper?

Disguise a hot pepper.

That's when it hit him, like a slap right to the side of his head. He had an idea, a *great* idea.

The question was whether he could actually do it,

especially onstage in front of a crowd, and in the time they'd given him. It was risky, the idea he had, but if he pulled it off, Max thought it could impress the judges and really be a winner.

We have to make our own rules, Master Plan had written to him.

Maybe this was part of that. Maybe he meant Max had to decide to take chances, even if they scared him.

Max decided to go for it.

Two hours later, he was standing in a row with the other kids trying out for the show, each of them holding a tray with what they'd made on it.

Max felt like he'd sweat through every inch of his clothes. His muscles were sore and his head hurt, but he'd done what he set out to do. He wasn't even sure how, really. He just did one thing, and then another, and then another, and didn't let himself stop.

The judges' table was set up between the first row of the audience and the front of the stage. Chef Luck, Aunt Lexi, and Zero Effect, in full superhero costume, sat behind the table, waiting.

"Before we start the judging," Bones Gormley said into his microphone, "how about a hand for our junior bakers here? This is a lot harder than it looks, folks!"

Everyone clapped. Max looked over and saw his mom

and Luca, who both looked to him like they were clapping the hardest.

He just hoped they couldn't see him sweating through his clothes.

Marina got judged before Max. She'd made mugs of hot, spicy chocolate cocoa from scratch, with jalapeño snicker-doodle cookies sitting on top of the mugs. The cookies were decorated beautifully with different colored frosting and little hot candy buttons she'd made herself, too.

The judges all agreed that Marina's cocoa had a little *too* much spice in it, but that her cookies were delicious and looked very presentable. She smiled the whole time, even when they told her what they didn't like.

It was weird. Max wasn't sure if he wanted her to win, or if he wanted himself to win.

"Thank you, Marina!" Bones Gormley said.

He motioned to Max.

"Max, please present your creation to our judges!"

Max took a deep breath and let it out as he walked forward, down the stage steps and up to the judge's table. He set his tray in front of them with shaking hands and then took three steps back.

None of them spoke at first. Max watched Chef Luck exchange what looked like confused looks with Aunt Lexi and Zero Effect.

"Uh, Max, my boy," Chef Luck began in his deep, booming voice. "Correct me if I'm wrong, but this looks exactly like the plate of peppers ol' Bones there gave y'all at the start of this thing."

He was right that they *looked* the same. There were six shiny green jalapeño-pepper-shaped things arranged on the tray in front of them, just the way Bones Gormley had presented the peppers to the kids when he revealed the secret ingredient for the challenge.

Max had to swallow hard before he was sure he could get words out of his mouth.

"I don't mean to correct you, Chef, but . . . you *are* wrong."

There was a bunch of murmuring in the crowd. The audience sounded confused.

Chef Luck, however, laughed out loud.

"I like this kid!" he proclaimed.

"Try one," Max urged the celebrity chef.

"All right, I will!"

Chef Luck picked up one of the "peppers," holding it between two thick fingertips. He opened his mouth and bit half of it off without fear.

After chewing for a few seconds, Chef Luck's eyes went wide and a big smile spread across his lips.

"Well, I'll be!" he announced. "The kid is right—it

ain't a pepper! It's a *brownie*! A caramel brownie, right?"

"Right," Max confirmed.

He wasn't ready for how relieved he felt that the judge knew what it was supposed to be, and that Chef Luck didn't spit out the brownie. Max's legs felt so weak that he wanted to drop to his knees.

The other two judges picked up a "pepper" for themselves and bit into them. They both looked just as surprised and happy as Chef Luck.

"Well, tell us how you did it, Max," Chef Luck urged him.

Max took in a deep, slow breath before he started talking.

"The jalapeño is chopped up and in the chocolate brownie," Max explained. "I made a bunch of molds by wrapping one of the actual peppers in aluminum foil, and then I cut the top off the foil and took the pepper out. I poured the brownie batter into the molds, and then stood them up by just kinda, like, sticking the tip of the bottoms of each mold into a baking rack. And then I baked them. I made a real simple caramel on the stove with cinnamon, and when the brownies were cool, I dipped them all in the caramel and waited for that to set. And then I painted them with those really cool, like, air guns you had back there for us. I used some of the molding chocolate from the pantry to make the part that looks like pepper stems, and I painted those darker green. And . . . and that's it."

"That is *darn* clever, Max!" Chef Luck said. "And these are darn tasty, too!"

The other judges looked genuinely impressed.

"Were you worried the caramel wouldn't set in time, Max?" Aunt Lexi asked him.

"Terrified," Max admitted, and everyone in the audience laughed.

"Well, the risk you took paid off. These belong in one of those videos where everything is cake. But they don't just look amazing; they taste wonderful. The balance between the peppers and the chocolate is perfect."

Zero Effect didn't really have anything to add to the discussion, but he did make one of the brownie peppers rise high into the air with his finger before letting it drop into his mouth.

Everyone laughed at that, too.

Max still thought he looked like a tool.

They judged the other two bakes. The big kid in the bow tie made a jalapeño flan with little cajeta candies on top of it. The tall girl had made a cool-looking tart with a bunch of different kinds of fruit mixed with the peppers, very bright and colorful. Max hated fruit pies and fruit tarts, though.

They liked everything and said nice stuff about the bakes, but none of the others got the reaction Max did.

Bones Gormley lined them up onstage again to wait for the judges to decide who the winner would be.

"That's so cool what you did," Marina whispered to him. "I can't even believe that. How did you come up with that?"

Max shrugged. "I just thought about me, kinda."

"What do you mean?"

He didn't answer her out loud, but in his head he thought, *I'm not what I look like, either.*

"All right!" Bones Gormley shouted, spreading his arms grandly. "The judges have conferred, and we have a winner. That talented young baker will be competing against the best junior bakers in the country on our show! Are you ready to find out who it is?"

"Good luck," he heard Marina whisper, and she sounded like she meant it.

"You too," he said.

When Bones Gormley said Max's name a few seconds later, Max didn't feel anything. He'd heard it. He understood that it meant he was the winner. He just wasn't ready.

Everything got very loud, but to Max it all sounded quiet for some reason. In fact, the only person he heard was Marina, who was smiling and clapping right next to him.

Eventually he felt Bones Gormley not all that gently pulling him forward from the rest of the kids by Max's shoulder. Max managed to smile and wave at the audience.

He remembered thinking he didn't need to win this contest.

What he knew in that moment was whether he needed to do it, he wanted it.

CONSOLATION PRIZES

"You deserved to win," Marina said.

"No way, you totally did!" Max insisted.

They were sitting together in chairs backstage while the film crew packed up their equipment. Bones Gormley had interviewed them both on camera, away from the crowd, after everything was over. He asked them about the challenge, what they'd done and how and why they'd done it, and how they felt about everything.

The conversation didn't make Max like the *Baked In* host any more than he had before, but at least Bones didn't make fun of him.

"You know, it's my birthday soon," Marina told him. "Like a week before you start doing the show, I think. I hope, anyway."

"You hope?"

"Yeah, I thought we could hang out. Maybe we can bake me a cake together or something."

"You mean, like, at your birthday party?"

Marina shook her head.

"I'm not having a birthday party this year."

"Why not?"

Marina looked down at her feet, swinging them back and forth and watching them disappear under her chair before reappearing.

"If it's none of my business, that's cool. I'm sorry."

She shook her head. "No, it's okay. It's just . . . without my dad around, it doesn't feel worth celebrating. I mean, I know it is, or whatever, but I don't *feel* like celebrating."

"I get that," Max said.

He thought it was weird and sad that Marina's dad would still be away on business during her birthday.

She was quiet for a minute, like she was thinking about something, and then she said, "Hey, can I tell you something?"

"Sure."

"I lied before. When I first told you why my dad isn't around. My dad isn't away on business. He's . . . he's in jail."

Max had no idea. None of the kids at school talked about it that he knew of. Marina must've been keeping it a secret, even from her friends.

"Oh. Wow. I'm really sorry, Marina."

"Your dad's not around either, is he?"

"Yeah, but that's different. He left when I was a baby."

"Do you still see him?"

Max shrugged. "Not really. But it doesn't bother me. I don't really know him."

"I thought I knew my dad, until he got arrested. I guess he was doing all this illegal business stuff."

"He was never bad to you, though, was he?"

"No. Never."

"People are complicated," Max said. "Being in jail doesn't mean your dad is a bad guy. I have a friend who's in jail."

"Oh, yeah? Who?"

"Just . . . he's, like, my uncle. Sort of. But he's not like they say he is."

"What did he do?"

"He . . . tried to fix something he thought was wrong. Just happened that the thing he thought was wrong was something the people who make the rules thought was right."

It was clear Marina didn't totally get what that was

supposed to mean, but she didn't question Max about it further.

"Well, anyway," she said. "We both know what it's like to have people we love miss our birthdays, I guess."

"But the difference is your dad *wants* to be with you, and he *can't*. That really sucks, but you gotta remember that part. He'd be here for your birthday if he could."

"Yeah, I know."

Max put on his best smile for her.

"I'd love to bake a cake with you for your birthday, though," he said. "We could make something awesome."

That seemed to make Marina happy.

"Sounds like a plan," she said.

From: 8mevojd@lightservice.net
To: maximus928@gmail.com
Subject: Marina

Maxwell,

Congratulations on your victory. It was well earned, by all accounts. I never had much talent in the kitchen, but if I were to seriously undertake cooking or baking, I would hope to become as clever as you.

I want to speak to you about this situation with Marina you described in your last email, concerning her birthday. It seems to me she is trying to hide from the world because of this situation with her father. That is understandable. However, hiding in such a way can be a bad thing, as you yourself know. Some things we have to face, and we are better for having faced them.

In my humble opinion, she *should* have her birthday party this year, and you should attend that party. It would be a good thing for both of you.

It would be a benefit to our work together for the rest of your classmates to see you and Marina together at such a party. It may, in fact, be the final piece of the puzzle we have been putting together since you first wrote to me.

It is clear Marina likes you and trusts you. You should

encourage her to go ahead with her party just as she would if her father were there.

Cordially,

Maximo

THINKING OUT LOUD

Max

Hey its Max

Marina

I know. I can see your name.

Oh right

Can I say something and I am not trying to tell you what to do or make you upset or whatever?

Sure

I think you should have your birthday party

Why? You don't want to hang out with me?

No I do! I was just thinking that I know you feel like it will make you sad but I know you are already sad and maybe being around people will help you feel better than you think that is all

I don't know Max

Like I said i am not trying to tell you what to do and i will totally come bake a cake with you i just want you to be happy and have a good birthday and i'm worried that not having your party will make you feel worse than you think having it will

My other friends said kind of the same thing as you

You must have smart friends then

So what do you think?

I still don't know

Tell you what

Have the party and if you are not having fun we can bail and go to a movie or something just us

How does that sound?

Okay deal

Max?

Yeah?

If I have fun at the party we can still go to a movie some time

Cool

I am just going to invite a few people tho to the party

Sounds good 👍

LEFT BEHIND

Max was in his room making sketches of what he was planning to make for Marina's party as her birthday gift. He had a million ideas, and he thought drawing it might help him sort them out.

"Max!" he heard his mom call to him from the living room. "Luca is here!"

Oh, crud, Max thought.

They were supposed to meet at the bookstore to scope the new comics that were out. They did it every week.

Max had completely blanked.

He felt like he'd been doing that a lot lately.

A few seconds later, Luca walked into his room and closed the door behind him.

"What the heck, dude?" Luca asked him. "I waited for you for like an hour."

"I'm sorry, man. I forgot."

Luca looked over the sketches spread across Max's bed.

"You entering an art contest now, too?"

"No, it's . . . Don't worry about it."

"'Don't worry about it.' Why do I feel like you never tell me anything anymore?"

"What are you even talking about?"

"All this stuff that's happening with you lately. That's happening to you. The way you look all different. Taking karate classes or whatever all the time. The Smoke coming to school. The TV show. You never say anything about any of it. It feels like there's stuff you don't tell me."

"You're the one who told me to enter the contest!" Max fired back at him.

"Yeah, well, I almost wish I hadn't. Like you needed another thing making you think you're the new king of the school."

"I don't think that! What's wrong with you?"

"What's wrong with *you*? I'm supposed to be your friend."

"How am I not treating you like my friend?"

"By leaving me behind! You know I can't buy new clothes. I can't cook stuff and have everybody treating me like a rock star. I can't pay to take karate classes. My parents can barely pay rent."

"It's not karate. It's Systema—"

"Whatever! You know what I'm saying!"

"It's not my fault your folks are having a hard time."

"It *is* your fault you decided to become some big hero without talking to me about any of it, and now you're treating me like your sidekick! I'm *not* your sidekick! I'm *nobody's* sidekick! I want to be somebody, too! I have stuff I'm good at, you know! Why do you get to be something and I . . . I . . . I can't . . ."

Luca looked like he was about to cry.

Max was stunned. He had no idea all of that had been building inside of his friend.

Before he could think of what to say, his mom was knocking at the door.

"Hey, is everything okay in there?"

"Yeah!" Max called to her automatically. "We're just talking!"

"All right," she said, sounding unsure. "Come out soon, and I'll make you guys a snack, okay?"

Max waited until he heard footsteps going away from his bedroom.

"I'm sorry, man," he said to Luca. "I'm really sorry. Okay? I mean it. You're right, I haven't been telling you everything that's going on. I don't think you're my side-kick, though. I know how smart you are. You're a lot smarter than me. It's not fair that everybody doesn't know that or can't see it. But I see it. I swear. I see you. You can do or be anything you want."

"I can't, though," Luca said quietly, staring down at the floor. "I can't be anything."

He was crying now. He almost melted down onto the end of Max's bed, sitting with his arms hanging down between his knees.

Max watched him, not sure what to do. He knew this was about more than their friendship.

Max walked over and sat down beside him. He knew what he wanted to do, but it was hard. He'd never hugged anyone except his mom and relatives before, and usually it was them hugging him.

Thinking about it, he wasn't sure he'd ever reached out to try to touch anyone before, for any reason.

Slowly, he put one arm around Luca's shoulders. He was worried for a second Luca might freak out and punch him or something, but he didn't.

It took a second, but Luca leaned against Max and let Max hold him. He squeezed his arm around Luca's shoulders tightly, leaning his cheek against the top of his friend's head.

"I didn't mean to yell at you," Luca said, snorting through his tears.

"Yeah, you did, but it's okay. I deserved it."

Luca laughed just a little bit. "Yeah, you did."

"I wanna tell you everything will be cool, but, like, I don't know that it will. I hope it will be. But I promise we'll still be friends and I won't treat you like you're . . . less than I am, or something. Okay? I *promise*."

Luca nodded, wiping his nose and mouth with the back of his arm.

"Thanks," he said softly.

Max could only nod. He felt uncomfortable, but he didn't want Luca to think he couldn't feel his feelings in front of Max.

"Hey," he said, gently shifting the subject to something more positive, "you're coming to Marina's party, right? We can roll in together. We can both act like big heroes."

Luca shook his head. "It's my dad's birthday, and then we're going to temple after. My mom wanted to take him out to a fancy dinner, but I guess we're doing this picnic in the park thing instead. Anyway. You're on your own, I guess."

"Great," Max said, not meaning it at all.

"You'll be fine," Luca assured him.

"Even without my sidekick?"

Luca laughed for real this time.

"You suck, dude," he said.

"I know. Thanks for being my best friend anyway."

"Yeah. Thanks for being mine."

They decided to go to the bookstore after all.

When Max came back that night, he wrote Master Plan an email about the whole thing.

CAKE WRECKS

Marina's house wasn't what Max expected.

He wasn't sure what he expected, exactly. When she messaged him her address, his mom had said something about it being in the "fancy" part of town, but he didn't think Marina lived in the biggest house he'd ever seen in real life. That's what it was, too. It was three floors, and the outside had more windows than Max had teeth. The front lawn looked like a park, with a huge circle for a driveway that could have hosted an entire parade.

"What . . . do her parents do for a living again?" his mom asked as she drove them around the circle.

"Her dad's in jail," Max said without thinking.

"For what?"

Max shrugged. "Business stuff."

His mom nodded knowingly. "That makes sense," she said. "They're lucky they still have the house. Usually the government takes that, too. When you get caught doing . . . business stuff."

Max nodded like he knew what any of that meant, even though he didn't.

He was still uncomfortable in the suit. It had arrived in a package addressed to him, just like the GoPro. He unpacked it and threw out the box and wrapping before his mom got home, and he had to tell her that he borrowed it from a cousin of Luca's (because nothing Luca wore would ever fit Max) just for the party.

She pulled the car in front of the steps that led up to the front doors (there were two of them). The whole thing looked like a courthouse on a TV show to Max.

"All right, call me if you want me to pick you up early, otherwise I'll see you at seven, okay?"

"Thanks, Mom."

"And have fun, okay?"

"Yeah," Max said, still feeling overwhelmed by the sight of Marina's home.

Max carefully lifted the pink cake box from the back seat of their car. His mom had gotten him the box specially. It was just like the ones you'd get at an actual bakery.

Inside was a birthday cake he'd made for Marina as his present to her. She loved peanut butter, she'd told him, so he found a recipe for a peanut butter and banana cake that looked good. He thought it would be cool to use each of their favorite flavors together.

He walked up the steps to the doors, but before he could knock or look for a doorbell, they seemed to open all on their own. A man wearing white gloves and a suit stepped out to greet him.

"Good afternoon, sir," he said to Max. "Are you an invited guest to Miss Marina's party?"

No one had ever called Max "sir" before.

"Uh, yeah," he said. "I guess I'm in the right place, then?"

The white-gloved man, who Max guessed was a butler, nodded by bowing his head low.

"Please follow me to the ballroom."

Max did as he was told, and he and his pink cake box walked inside the house, feeling horribly out of place. The floor was shiny marble, and his shoes made loud sounds as he walked across it. There was a giant staircase that went up to the second floor, and another giant staircase that came back down from the second floor.

The butler didn't lead him up the stairs. Instead they walked to the side of the staircases, toward doors even taller than the ones out front. Max could hear hip-hop music playing on the other side. The white-gloved man pulled open one of the doors and motioned Max to walk through them.

The "ballroom" looked as big as their school auditorium to Max. The ceiling was just as high. It looked like their entire school was there. It was weird that even the seventh and eighth graders were invited, let alone showed up, for a sixth-grade girl's birthday party. But this wasn't any ordinary kid's birthday party, Max guessed.

It was more like a carnival, really. There were even rides. They'd set up a small go-cart track in the very middle of the room with tiny cars you could actually drive around it. Kids were yelling and laughing as they raced each other. There was a whole laser tag maze. People in weird costumes were walking around the party doing things like juggling bowling pins and blowing giant bubbles through huge rings and one of them was on giant stilts that made him fifteen feet tall.

It looked like they had any kind of food you could want. There was a guy with a hot dog cart. There was another booth making tacos and hand-making the tortillas. They had a big machine making ice cream, and another machine rolling out hot doughnuts on a conveyor belt. There was a fountain of pouring chocolate that was taller than Max, with all kinds of things around it to dip in the chocolate, like marshmallows and strawberries and cookies.

There was a DJ playing loud music, but Max could barely see him with all the equipment he had set up. It looked like the cockpit of a spaceship, with flashing lights and tower speakers of futuristic-looking metal.

It wasn't like any party Max had ever been to. Although the truth was, this was also the first party Max had ever been to (not counting adult parties hosted by his mom).

"Max!"

It was Marina. She practically skipped across the room to him, smiling. She was wearing a bright yellow dress and had her long black hair pinned up. She looked the prettiest Max had ever seen her.

"Man, you really went for it, huh?" Max said, still trying to take everything in.

Marina shrugged, still smiling brilliantly.

"I just took your advice, that's all."

Advice can be dangerous.

It was his thought, but Max heard it in Master Plan's voice. Maximo had never written those words to him, that he could remember.

Max wasn't sure why he thought that. He just had a weird feeling inside, like when you are staring down a dark alley at night, thinking about walking into it.

"Don't, like, take this the wrong way," Max said, looking around again at how big and impressive everything around him was, "but shouldn't you be going to a . . . nicer school than ours?"

Marina looked embarrassed. She even blushed a little.

"Dad always said he didn't want me growing up to be a spoiled rich kid. Oh, hey, speaking of my dad!"

She grabbed him by the arm and pulled him along through the sea of other kids. Max gripped his cake box tightly, trying to keep it steady and level so the inside of the box didn't mess up the frosting.

"Look! That's my dad! They let him out just for the day to come to my party!"

Marina pointed at one of the many tables set up around the walls of the room for people to sit and eat at.

Marina's father was a handsome older man wearing a fancy-looking suit. A woman Max guessed was Marina's mom was feeding him a chocolate-covered strawberry. They both looked really happy.

Other men in suits surrounded the table he was sitting at, only their suits didn't look nearly as fancy. They were plain and as black as the sunglasses they all wore, even though they were all inside a house. And each one of them had one of those earpieces like spies in a movie.

"That's why there's so many people," Marina explained. "I didn't mean to invite the whole school, but when dad found out he was going to get to be here, he wanted to make it big. That's just how he is."

"Who are those other guys?" Max asked Marina.

"Oh. They're, like, guards?"

"Like security guards?"

"Kind of. They're not guarding my dad from other people, though. They . . . they're making sure he doesn't go anywhere."

"Oh. So they're, like, police."

"Kind of, yeah."

"Sorry."

The smile returned to Marina's face.

"It's okay. I'm just happy he's here. And it's all because of you! Thank you so much!"

Max was going to say that he didn't really do anything, just encouraged her to have the party she wanted to have.

"Hey, is that for me?" Marina asked, looking at the box in his hands.

"Yeah. I . . . I mean, I know you already have a cake. But I made you one. Special."

"Omigod, thank you, that's so sweet! I'll have them put it on the dessert table right now! I'll bet it's awesome!"

She took the box from him excitedly.

Max didn't know what to do. He'd already been nervous enough about hanging out with her around other kids, like her friends. Having every grade of their school there didn't make it any easier.

Before he could think of what else to say, though, Marina leaned up and kissed him on the cheek.

"Have fun, okay? We'll hang later. I have to keep saying hi to people. I really didn't think, like, the whole school would come. But like I said, Daddy made me invite everyone. He was so excited."

Max reached up and rubbed his cheek, nodding at her.

His mouth felt dry, and he didn't trust himself to talk just then.

Marina didn't seem to notice. She skipped away just as she'd skipped over to him, and soon she was lost in the big crowd.

Max didn't know what to do at first. He wished Luca had been there. His friend was invited, just like the rest of their school, but today was his dad's birthday.

Fortunately, Luca wasn't the only sixth grader who knew him or wanted to hang out with him anymore. Max soon found out that their entire class knew his name, and when they saw him alone, several of them came up to him and invited him to join them for laser tag. They all congratulated him on winning a spot on *Baked In Junior* and told him how awesome his fake pepper brownies were.

The laser tag vest barely fit him, but nobody said anything about it. They played three rounds, and in the first, Max got killed right away, but he did better the more he played.

Afterward he was tired and hungry and thirsty. Max was thinking about attacking the dessert table, but he was always afraid to eat around so many people, especially sweets or any kind of junk food. When you were fat, they always looked at you like you were doing something wrong when you ate that kind of stuff in public.

He was staring at the cake when he caught sight of several tall figures walking toward him out the corner of his eye and turned around.

All thoughts of food left him.

It was Johnny Pro, and he wasn't alone. Three of the biggest kids on the water polo team were surrounding him.

And they were all headed straight for Max.

"We got your message, double-wide," Johnny Pro said to him.

Max's heart was beating really fast, but he was surprised by how unafraid of the older boy and his friends he was. Usually he would've been a wreck as soon as Johnny Pro even looked at him.

"What are you talking about?" Max asked.

Johnny Pro held up his phone. On the screen was a group text that Max could only guess had all the water polo team guys on it. There was a message that read: *This is Max. None of you better show up at Marina's party, or I'm going to mess you up bad. Believe it.*

Max had to read it twice before it really sunk in that Johnny Pro thought this was a message from him.

"I didn't send you that!"

Johnny Pro laughed.

"Right. You didn't send it, or you didn't think we'd show up? I guess you don't remember me telling you what would happen the next time I saw you outside school, either?"

"Look, I'm sorry about what happened to you, getting suspended and kicked off the team, but it wasn't my fault, okay?"

Except it *was* his fault, of course. He'd masterminded the whole thing. Max remembered when telling the smallest lie to his mom made his stomach twist up.

Lying wasn't hard for him anymore. It was easy. He just had to want whatever the lie was going to get him bad enough.

What Max wanted in that moment, more than anything, was for Johnny Pro and his friends to just walk away. He wasn't afraid of Johnny Pro anymore, or what the older boy might do to him. He just didn't want to cause any problems at Marina's party, especially with her dad there. It was about more than just wanting her to like him. Max knew how much this day meant to her, and he didn't want to see it get spoiled.

Johnny Pro wasn't worried about any of that, though.

"You think you're such hot stuff now, don't you? With your stupid new clothes and glasses and your stupid hair and getting your hand slapped by The Smoke. You think I don't see you? *You* shouldn't even be here."

Johnny Pro shoved him, pushing both of his strong hands against Max's chest and backing him up several steps. It didn't hurt, but it changed something inside of Max suddenly. He wasn't sure if it was all the training he'd been doing with Gunnar, or if it was everything else he'd done to act and feel different about himself.

Whatever it was, Max didn't want them to go away and leave him alone anymore. He forgot all about Marina and her party and his plans. He wanted to show Johnny Pro that Max wasn't the fat kid from the beginning of the year. He wasn't their punching bag anymore.

He wanted to show them all that he was as bad as a supervillain.

Max spread his feet apart and bent his knees just a little. It felt natural after all the times Gunnar had made him do it.

Johnny Pro stepped forward to shove him again. Max

could see the former water polo team captain's feet. The older boy put his right foot forward way too far. Max knew from training with Gunnar that Johnny Pro was off balance, standing like that.

Max took a step forward at the same time and raised his arms, just a little. He let each of Johnny Pro's hands slide under one of Max's raised arms. When Max dropped his arms, he had both of Johnny Pro's wrists trapped. Then all Max had to do was turn his own body, exactly the way he'd been taught to do.

He didn't try to move Johnny Pro at all. It was like the other boy wasn't even there. But as Max turned, he took Johnny Pro's wrists and arms with him. Johnny Pro had already put himself off balance when he moved forward to shove Max. Surprise and momentum did the rest.

First Johnny Pro stumbled, and then he fell. Max raised his arms again and released the older boy's wrists. Johnny Pro went crashing and rolling across the floor, away from him.

Max couldn't believe he'd just done that as he looked down at the older boy.

He looked up just in time to see the other three eighth graders charging at him in an angry wave of bodies. Max didn't have time to panic or get scared. He didn't have time to think at all. Everything he and his instructor had been teaching his muscles took over. His body seemed like it was moving all by itself.

Max ran back at them, and just as they were about to collide, he dropped to his knees and rolled forward into their legs. Two of the boys tripped over him and each other. They went flying, falling hard onto the floor next to Johnny Pro.

When Max got back to his feet, the boy who was still standing threw a punch at Max's face. Max didn't duck or try to move out of the way. Instead he dropped his chin to his chest and leaned the top of his head into the punch. The very top part of your head is a lot harder than most people realize.

It hurt Max when the boy's fist hit him, but the top of his head hurt the boy's fist a lot more. The eighth grader jumped back, holding his hand against his chest and yelling in pain.

Max tried to catch his breath and then realized he wasn't breathing all that hard.

At least, not until he turned and saw Johnny Pro standing back up, his eyes practically burning as he looked at Max.

It was just the two of them now.

The boy who had made him afraid to get out of bed every morning had his fists raised like a boxer. It was the same way he'd looked every time he teed off on Max to amuse his friends.

Max thought about all those times Gunnar had poked him with the stick, teaching him to be aware of attacks coming at him from any angle, whether he could see them or not.

Johnny Pro started firing punches at Max's body. The ones Max didn't dodge outright only managed to glance off him harmlessly. He backed up toward the dessert table slowly, moving away as the bully kept stepping toward him throwing fist after fist.

After a while, Johnny Pro stopped swinging his arms. He looked tired and out of breath, but even angrier than before.

Finally, Johnny Pro let out a loud, furious yell and threw a wild roundhouse punch aimed right at the middle of Max's face. If it connected, it surely would have taken Max's whole head off.

Max stepped forward just as he had when the older boy tried to shove him. This time Max caught Johnny Pro's wrist by pressing it between the side of Max's face and his shoulder. Max spun around as fast as he could. As he turned, pulling Johnny Pro with him again, he let his whole body drop to the floor. That sent Johnny Pro flying even faster and higher all the way over the top of Max.

He didn't hear the crash. It was like watching a scene from a movie in slow motion. Johnny Pro's whole body fell on top of the middle of the table, right onto the cake Max had made for Marina's birthday. The cake exploded, and the entire table collapsed in a thunderous boom, sending strawberries and cookies and sprays of chocolate flying in every direction.

That stopped the entire party dead. The music was gone. Every pair of eyes was now looking at Max and the chaos he had created.

The men in dark suits and darker glasses, the ones who'd been guarding Marina's father like he was the president, swooped in all around Max. One of them grabbed Johnny Pro in a headlock as the boy tried to climb through the wreckage of the table to come at Max again. He got smashed cake and frosting all over the man's suit. The others were wrangling the two boys Max had tripped, who had recovered behind him and still wanted to fight.

None of the guards came near Max or even looked at him. It was probably because Max wasn't yelling or running around or causing a fuss. He just stood there, with a calm look on his face.

"Max! What did you do?"

Marina was there, in her bright yellow dress. She looked

even angrier than Johnny Pro had when he tried to knock Max's head off.

It all came back to him then. He remembered where he was and what he was trying to do. He remembered how he hadn't wanted to ruin Marina's party, which is exactly what he'd just done.

"Hey!" one of the guards shouted at the others. "Where's the target?"

He pointed. Everyone around seemed to look to where he was pointing at the same time, including Max.

The chair Marina's father had been sitting in at the table was empty.

Her mother was still there. She stared back at them all with her lips tight and a hard look in her eyes.

She didn't say anything.

Suddenly all the men in dark sunglasses didn't care about Johnny Pro and his friends anymore. They let the water polo players go and ran back through the crowd, shoving people out of the way roughly.

"Daddy?" Marina whispered quietly beside Max, not really talking to anybody except herself.

Max didn't understand what was happening.

"He's gone!" he heard one of the guards yelling.

Max could see them talking into their earpieces.

"We have lost the prisoner! I repeat, we have lost the

prisoner! Alert local authorities!"

"Let's lock this place down!" another one of the guards yelled. "Nobody move!"

Marina began to cry. They weren't small, quiet tears either.

When she looked at him again, her eyes were red and wet, and her lips were trembling.

"You ruined everything," she told him.

It hurt worse than letting Johnny Pro's whole team hold Max down and beat him into tiny bits ever could have.

He tried to think of something, anything to say to her that would somehow make this better.

Before he could get a single word out, Marina's mother came and swept her away.

Max reached out a hand uselessly, but in seconds, they both disappeared into the crowd and were gone.

He looked from where he'd watch her disappear past the sea of guests to where Johnny Pro was lying helpless in a puddle of decimated desserts.

Max was standing, and Johnny Pro was curled up on the floor, beaten and humiliated. They all were.

He'd imagined versions of this a thousand times in his head, and now that it had actually happened, it didn't feel anything like he thought, like he expected.

It felt terrible.

He felt terrible.

Max had gotten his revenge, and he didn't want it. He didn't want any of it. All he wanted was to take back the last five minutes of his life.

MAKE-UP BAKE-UP

"**D**ude, you *wrecked* their butts! This is the greatest thing I've ever seen in my whole entire life!"

Luca was watching the clip for the tenth or eleventh time in a row on Max's mom's laptop.

"Will you stop it?" Max asked, already way past being annoyed with his friend.

They were in Max's kitchen a few days after the party. Max was mixing sugar and butter and peanut butter in his mom's food processor. He was determined to make Marina another cake as an apology for what happened.

At least twenty different kids who were at the party recorded the fight on their phones and posted it to YouTube. It wasn't getting as many views as the video of Johnny

Pro bullying him and Luca had, at least not yet, but it was getting around.

He was only a little worried about what The Smoke would think if he saw it.

Luca was practically cheering by the end of his latest viewing of the video. "I mean, I know you've learned a lot of cool moves and stuff, but I didn't know you were, like, John Wick now!"

"Will you knock it off, Luca?"

"I'm just saying, man! You're like a superhero now!"

Max dropped the spatula in his hand to the counter with a loud clatter.

"I am not a *superhero*. I *hate* those jerks. *All* of them.

Luca backed off quickly. "All right, calm down. I'm just saying."

But Max wasn't about to let it go.

"You know what, though? You're right. It was like a superhero, because I wrecked everything, and instead of being mad about all the stuff I wrecked, everyone is happy because I beat up a few jackholes. That's exactly like a superhero. You're right."

Luca looked confused.

"Why are you getting so mad?"

"It wasn't cool, man. I wrecked Marina's whole birthday. She *hates* me now."

"She'll get over it."

"You don't know that."

"If you made me a cake, I'd get over it. You make good cakes."

"I was already gonna give you the leftover frosting. You don't have to suck up to me."

Max hadn't written Master Plan about the party yet. He didn't know exactly why. Normally it would've been the first thing he did when he got home.

It wasn't that he didn't want to admit it to Master Plan that things went badly. Something just felt off, in a way Max couldn't give a name to.

But baking this make-up cake for Marina was the first thing he'd done on his own without Master Plan's advice since they started writing to each other. Max kept thinking about that as he continued making his frosting.

"I hate that I had to be at temple that day," Luca was complaining. "I swear, I would've been right in there with you, throwing hands like Conor McGregor."

Luca threw a few half-speed punches at the air in front of him, making mean faces and movie fight sound effects with his mouth.

Max wanted to tell him the way he was moving was wrong, but the last time he tried to teach him something like that it hadn't ended well.

"Just click out of that video, okay? I don't want my mom walking in and seeing it."

"She seriously doesn't know about the fight?"

"She knows Marina's dad got away from the police and they had to ask us all a bunch of questions. That's all."

"Did the cops blame you?"

Max stopped what he was doing.

"What? Why would they blame *me*?"

Luca looked at him oddly, like he couldn't believe Max had to ask.

"I mean, all those cops who were guarding her dad only got distracted because you dunked Johnny Pro through the cake table. I'm not, like, saying it's your fault or anything. I just wondered."

Max stared at Luca in stunned silence. He hadn't thought about that. Neither had any of the adults at the party. No one who questioned him about Marina's dad escaping had said a word to him about the fight. They must have thought it was just an accident, kids being kids.

Because that's what it was, right? Max asked himself. *It was just a thing that happened. It didn't have anything to do with Marina's dad running away.*

Luca was still watching him. "You really didn't think about that, huh?"

Max shook his head slowly.

Luca grinned. "Like I always say, dumbest smart kid I know."

"I guess so," Max said.

He decided he didn't want to think about it anymore right then. He just wanted to finish his cake and take it over to Marina's house and find out if she was okay, and also maybe, possibly, ask if she would forgive him.

But mostly it was the finding-out-if-she-was-okay part.

Mostly.

NOBODY HOME

For the second time, Max carefully lifted a cake box out of the back seat of his mom's car in front of Marina's giant house.

"Do you want me to come up with you, honeybun?" his mom asked.

"Please, please never call me that again," he grumbled at her. "I hate it."

She frowned at him. "Don't get snippy with me, mister. I know you're having a rough week and you're upset about this thing with Marina, but things happen. Her dad being a fugitive has nothing to do with you."

I'm not totally sure about that, Max thought.

"Sorry," he said instead.

Max shut the back door of the car and walked up the steps to the big front doors. This time, however, no butler opened them.

He tried knocking, but then he thought knocking was dumb in a place this gigantic. No one would hear it unless they were standing right on the other side of the doors.

He looked for a button and found one, set in the middle of a gold circle, near the doors. When he pushed it, he heard loud, musical bells chime inside the house.

Max waited. He looked down for a second and thought he remembered there being a big, colorful doormat there the last time. Now there was nothing, just cement.

After what felt like two minutes, Max rang the doorbell again. He was starting to feel sweaty.

No one answered the door.

Max walked around to the nearest window and peeked inside. He didn't spot anyone moving around. He also noticed that a lot of stuff he'd seen the first time he'd been in Marina's house seemed like it was missing. Paintings had been taken down off the walls. Vases and statues were gone from the little side tables in the marble-floored room between the stairs.

It was like they'd moved or something.

It looked a *lot* like they'd moved, actually.

That didn't make any sense, though. This house had

only just been filled with hundreds of people. It was Marina's home. Besides, if they'd left, with her dad on the run from the police, how would he know where they'd be when he wanted to talk to them again?

Max didn't know what else to do. He left the cake on the doorstep, setting the box down carefully on the dust-lined spot where the welcome mat used to be.

He didn't say anything when he climbed back into the passenger seat of the car.

"Nobody was home?" his mom asked.

Max didn't answer at first.

"Honeybu— . . . Max? They weren't there?"

"Nope," he said, trying to sound normal. "Nobody's home."

Dear Max,

I am really sorry for how I acted and what I said to you at my party. I didn't mean it. And I know what happened was not your fault. I knew Johnny and those other jerks would start trouble. That is why I didn't invite them. I don't know how they got in. I swear. Everyone I invited was on a list our butler had on his iPad. He wasn't supposed to let anyone not on the list in. But they got what they deserved as far as I am concerned. I wish I could ask you where you learned how to fight like that though, because it was amazing.

I am not going to see you at school again. I should not be telling you any of this, but I wanted to say that I was sorry, and I wanted to explain so you would understand. I really like you. I am sorry we will not get to see each other more and be friends.

My dad had to leave my party because it was his only chance to escape. He said he would have spent the rest of his life in jail if he hadn't done it.

He sent for us secretly, but we have to go right now, or we might not be able to get to him.

I can't tell you where we are going. I know you will understand that. I can tell you Dad says we are going to have a new home far away from here, where no one will bother us. He will be doing important work for someone he met in jail. But I don't think we will ever come back.

I don't know if my dad is a bad person. I just know he is my dad and I love him, and my mom and me want to be together. I hope that makes sense to you.

Thank you for my cake. I am sorry I didn't get to eat it.

You are a good guy, Max. You were a good friend when I needed one. Thank you.

Best wishes,
Marina
xxxooxxx

GONE

The letter from Marina came a few days after Max dropped off his apology cake at her empty house. He had to read it four times before he finally started to really understand what it meant.

He was struck again by how she had really nice handwriting, way better than his. The way she signed her name with the little *x*'s and *o*'s made him smile, made him feel good inside, and then made him incredibly sad. Max watched as a tiny drop of water fell onto the piece of paper, between the parts where she talked about what a good guy he was, and he realized he'd started crying.

He couldn't believe he'd never see Marina again. They'd just become friends and maybe even more, exactly like he'd wanted. Now that was over.

It all felt like it was for nothing, everything he'd done over the past few months, and everything he'd learned. Setting up Johnny Pro and taking him down, changing all the things Max didn't like about himself, getting into the contest and winning and making the whole school know who he was and like him. When the year started, Max couldn't have a better fantasy or dream than beating up half the water polo team in front of his entire class, and now he didn't care that he'd done it.

He didn't even want to go on the dumb *Baked In Junior* show now. The thought of having to do that all over again, but this time on TV in front of the whole world, was terrifying.

What are you talking about? What is wrong with you?

The question bubbled up in his brain out of nowhere.

Why are you thinking like the old you? Why do you want to go back to being scared all the time and feeling like nothing matters?

Before, that voice in his head sounded like Master Plan.

Now it sounded like Max, talking to himself.

You didn't write to Master Plan and ask for his help and take all his advice just to make Marina like you, and you know it. Stop feeling sorry for yourself! You can be whatever you want and do whatever you want. You proved that. What more do you need?

That was true. It *hadn't* all been about a girl. He really did like Marina a lot, and he thought he would have gotten to like her even more if they'd been able to keep spending time together. He was sad she was gone.

But the more Max thought about it, the more he had to admit that the truth was, he didn't really know Marina when he started writing to Master Plan.

He knew she was pretty, and he thought she had a kind smile. That was all. He understood now that he'd just liked the *idea* of Marina, of talking to a girl and having her like him back, and maybe even being his girlfriend someday. His whole life until now, he'd never thought that could ever happen.

But wanting all of that was a lot different than liking a person because of who they are. He knew the difference now.

Still, it hurt.

"Max!" his mom called to him from the living room. "Luca's here!"

Max quickly folded up the letter and stashed it under his pillow. He tried to wipe the tears away without rubbing his eyes, because he didn't want them make them any redder.

"Okay!"

Luca came running into Max's room a minute later, already out of breath. He was carrying Max's mom's laptop, which was open to some webpage.

"Dude, check this out! I heard about it on TV and I had to come tell you!"

Luca stopped running, and his excitement faded when he looked at Max.

"Oh. Are you okay?"

"Yeah, why?"

"You just . . . you look like you were crying."

Max was going to lie or make up some excuse about why his eyes were red and wet.

"Yeah, I was crying," he said instead. "I'm fine, though."

Max figured Master Plan would have told him not to apologize for crying, and not to be embarrassed about it. And he'd be right, Max thought.

Besides, Max was tired of being embarrassed and ashamed of himself. He'd decided that was over.

"You're sure you're okay?" Luca asked, looking genuinely concerned for his friend.

"Yeah. What do you want to show me?"

"Uh, yeah. I saw this and I thought of you, 'cuz of that letter you wrote him that he answered."

"Who?"

"Your favorite. Master Plan."

Luca showed him the laptop screen. It was an article from a news website with a story about Master Plan. The article said that Master Plan was going to get a new trial.

Max blinked. Maximo hadn't written anything about that to him.

The article explained that if Master Plan was found to be innocent at the end of this new trial, they would let him out of jail free and clear. The reason they were giving him another trial for the same crime he'd already been declared guilty of was because new evidence had been found. Apparently there was a video of Cobalt, the superhero Max couldn't stand who'd captured Master Plan. They didn't say exactly what was on the video, but they did say there were rumors that it might show Cobalt taking money from a rich businessman to do something illegal.

Cobalt wasn't just the one who captured Master Plan, he was the one and only witness who testified that Master Plan committed the crimes that ended up sending him to jail; the video might make a judge question whether they could trust Cobalt's testimony. If that was true, then the judge would have to set Master Plan free.

The article said that the video had been sent to the authorities "anonymously," which meant they didn't know who gave it to them. No one was taking credit for it.

Max knew one thing for sure right away. The video couldn't have come from Master Plan himself. If Maximo had that video, he would've shown it to them the minute

Cobalt took him in, before they sent him to jail.

"Isn't that bananas?" Luca asked. "What if Cobalt really is a bad guy?"

"They're all bad guys," Max said, but he was barely paying attention to Luca.

Max was thinking about what Marina said, about her dad being in jail, that he was arrested for doing "business stuff."

Max picked up the laptop and sat back in his bed, placing it on his lap so that Luca couldn't see the screen anymore. He typed Marina's father's name into the internet search engine and hit the "enter" key.

"What's up?" Luca asked, watching Max curiously.

"I just want to see something. Hold on."

There were dozens of news articles that came up about Marina's dad escaping from federal marshals at his daughter's birthday party. Max clicked on the first one he saw. It talked about how Marina's dad was a "fixer" for rich people and criminal organizations. He solved problems his bosses couldn't go to the police about, because those problems all had to do with breaking the law. The way Marina's dad fixed those problems was by bribing people with money, or blackmailing them with secrets he found out about them, and sometimes if neither of those worked, he did even worse things.

Sure enough, a few sentences later, it mentioned the prison where Marina's dad had been placed while he was waiting for his own trial.

It was the same prison where Master Plan was being held.

Max read down to the bottom of the article, where it was written that the police had questioned Marina's dad's cellmate in the jail, who was the notorious supervillain Maximo Marconius III, also known as Master Plan.

He and Marina's dad hadn't just been in the same prison; they had shared a cell together.

Max's stomach began to hurt, bad. He felt that fizzing on top of his brain again. He thought about the message Johnny Pro had showed him at Marina's party, the one that was supposed to be from Max, calling out the whole water polo team. He really hadn't sent them that message. Why would he? He would have to be crazy to challenge a squad of eighth graders like that. With everything that had happened since the party, Max had forgotten about that whole part.

Marina had written in her letter that she hadn't invited them to her party, either. She said they would have had to be on a list that was on an iPad.

iPads were all connected to the internet, Max thought.

"You think they'll let him out?" Luca asked.

Max looked up from the screen, his brain still fizzing. "Huh? Who?"

"Master Plan. Do you think they'll let him out of jail?"

Max didn't answer him, but he was pretty sure they would.

They would let him out, because that's how Master Plan had set things up.

Luca was watching him curiously. "What's wrong? I thought this would make you happy. He's your favorite."

That was true, wasn't it?

Max always liked the villains more than the heroes because they were all more like him. He also liked them because he thought they were more honest about who they were and what they did and why they did it than the heroes ever were.

He'd never questioned whether Master Plan was telling him the truth or not. Max thought they were the same.

He saw now that he'd been wrong about that.

Max set the laptop on the bed next to him and scooted forward to face Luca.

"There's a lot of stuff that's been going on the past few months," Max said, "that I haven't told you about, because I didn't think I could, or that you'd understand. I'm sorry I thought that. I don't want to lie to you. I don't want to lie to anybody."

"Okay, man. You can tell me."

Max did. He told Luca everything. He even read him all the emails Max had exchanged with Master Plan.

It had been fun keeping that secret. It had been fun being Master Plan's partner in crime. It had been fun feeling like a supervillain.

Max didn't want to feel that way anymore.

From: maximus928@gmail.com
To: 8mevojd@lightservice.net
Subject: Heroes and Villains

Maximo,

I have decided this is the last email I am ever going to write you, and I am not opening any more emails you send me.

I know what you did, and I know why you did it. At least, I think I do. You made a deal with Marina's dad, didn't you? He was your cellmate. He had something that could help you get a new trial and maybe get out of jail. That's what he does. He finds out secrets and bribes people, even superheroes. So you helped him escape. You used me to do it. You told me to convince Marina to have her party so that they would let her dad out to go to it. You sent invitations to Johnny Pro and his friends, and you must have hacked the list of guests and put them on it so Marina's butler would let them in. You sent that message to Johnny Pro and the water polo team that was supposed to be from me so that they would get mad and come after me at the party. You got me all those lessons from Gunnar so that I could fight back and those policemen guarding

Marina's dad would have to break up the fight and give him his chance to get away from them.

It was a great plan. It worked perfectly. At least I know I picked the right guy to ask for help.

I guess Marina's dad is going to be working for you now, right? She wrote me a letter that said he is going to be doing important work for somebody he met in jail. And someone like you can probably really use someone like him. If so, that might mean you will get to see Marina, even though I never will again.

I don't think it was an accident that Marina ended up in that *Baked In Junior* contest with me, either. You promised you didn't help me win, but did you help her get in so we'd be on that stage together? I think you probably did.

I keep trying to figure out and decide if you had all of this planned from the first time you emailed me, or if you figured out later that you could use me to help yourself.

(You don't need to answer any of that. Like I said, I am not going to read it.)

It does not really matter either way, I guess. But of course you probably did know right from the start. It is right there in your name, isn't it? And I knew that. I knew who you were when I wrote you that first letter.

You told me one time that I have to make up my own rules. You were right, but you were wrong, too. I have to figure out which rules are good and which are bad. People, I think, made some rules so that they can control other people. Some rules hurt people. But some rules are good. Some rules are there for a reason.

You have to decide if a rule hurts other people who aren't you. That's what makes a rule good or bad.

I don't think you care what your rules do to other people, as long as you get what you want. I think that because that is exactly how I started to feel inside, too. I started not to care about lying or cheating as long as it helped me win.

You know when I was the most like you? It wasn't all the stuff we planned and that I pulled off with your help. I was the most like you when I threw Johnny Pro into that cake table. I told Luca that was something a big dumb superhero would do, but it is also something you would do. It's something you made me do for you.

Superheroes and supervillains aren't the same all the time, but they are the same when they decide it doesn't matter if what they do hurts other people as long as they win.

I think regular people are the same way. I don't want to hurt other people. I'm not just talking about bullies like Johnny Pro. And I don't just mean beating up some dumb kids. I'm talking about Marina, how I hurt her by messing up her birthday. I'm talking about Luca, how he got hurt trying to help me without even knowing it was part of yours and my plan. I'm talking about people like me, who bigger kids don't think matter.

You taught me a lot of things, but the biggest thing you have taught me is that I don't want to be like you, not really.

I have to say thank you to you, though, because you did help me, a lot, even if you only did it to help yourself. That is why I can't be mad at you, or at least not really mad. I just know that I can't be your friend.

I would tell you that I hope you change, but I know that you won't. So instead I just hope you don't get caught next time, and that whatever you do doesn't wreck things for other people too bad.

Sincerely,

Maxwell Tercero

From: 8mevojd@lightservice.net
To: maximus928@gmail.com
Subject: RE: Heroes and Villains

Maxwell,

I believe you when you say that you will not be opening any more messages from me, but I am choosing to write this reply anyway, in the hopes that you might read it. Perhaps you will see this as the gesture I mean it to be, and know that despite everything, I do care for and about you. I care very much, in fact.

Everything you wrote is correct. I did exactly what you think I did. It's funny; usually when someone figures out one of my plans, I find it very troublesome. I even get angry. I am proud of you, however.

Did I plan to use you from the very beginning? Did I only agree to help you so that I could put my own plan in motion? As you say, it doesn't really matter, does it? I made a choice. My choice was to take advantage of our friendship and your trust in order to help free myself from my captivity and to exact my revenge on that bumbling, corrupt idiot who put me in prison in the first place. It doesn't matter when I decided to do that. It only matters that I did.

As I have told you before, Maxwell, we cannot act against our natures. We cannot go against what we are. I will always choose my own interests and desires over other people. It doesn't

252

matter how much I like them or respect those people. I will always come first. That is my nature.

Perhaps that, more than anything else, more than any laws I have broken, is what makes me a villain.

Your nature is different, my young friend. I knew from the first letter you wrote me that you could never be me; you could never truly be a villain. You care about other people. I did consider letting you in on the final part of my plan, but I knew you would not agree to do what I needed you to do. You cared about Marina and her happiness too much to disrupt her party and ruin her big day, even if I'd asked you to do so.

I do not blame you for this, or see it as a failure on your part. It is a good thing. I wish more superheroes were like you. I truly do.

If I may, I would like to give you one final piece of advice. I of course would not blame you if you chose to no longer take my advice, but I feel this is important for you to know.

The only problem you ever truly had, Maxwell, was that you were waiting. That is why you wrote to me and why you felt you needed me.

You never needed me to tell you what to do. You are a bright, clever, strong young person. You had everything within you to make the changes you wanted to make for yourself and about yourself.

It is difficult being young. I think because when we are young we feel so powerless. You feel as though you have no control over anything, even yourself. Adults rarely understand the difference between teaching a child what they need to know and controlling everything a child does. Somehow, adults only remember how much they did not know when they were children. They forget all the things they *did* know, and they forget how early they knew them.

At some point, Maxwell, you have to decide to stop waiting, for adults or for anyone else your age. As you say, perhaps some rules are good, and they are there for a reason. I am not saying you should not follow those rules. I am saying you have to stop waiting for other people to tell you what to do. You have to stop waiting for other people to tell you how and who to be. You have to stop waiting for other people to give you permission to live your life.

I hope you can understand what I mean. Do not worry if you don't understand it right now, however. I have every confidence that you will, in time.

Until then, stay true to your nature.

I wish you the best. Thank you for all you have done for me. I may have taught you many things, but I promise that you taught me just as much in return.

I remain . . .

Your friend,
Maximo

LIGHTS, CAMERA, ACTION

Max knew other people didn't sweat like this, and for what must have been the millionth time in his life, he hated that he wasn't one of those people.

"Isn't this *exciting*?" his mom whispered behind him.

It should've been. They were in a real television studio, and he was about to walk onto the set of *Baked In Junior* to compete in what would hopefully be the first of several episodes (if he won today, anyway).

Not only that, but an entire field trip of kids from his school had come to be in the audience for the recording of the episode. There were bleachers like in the school gym, facing the kitchen set. The seats were filled with maybe a couple hundred people, and dozens of them were from

Captain Clobbertime Memorial Middle School.

He wanted to be more excited, but Max just felt nervous. Not so much scared, he realized, just very anxious, like he wanted to get started so he didn't have to think about it anymore.

The other contestants and their parents were lined up beside him, just off the kitchen set. He'd been introduced to all of them before and they seemed cool, or at least they were nice.

There was a woman wearing a headset with a microphone attached to it. She was carrying a tablet and introduced herself as the set manager.

"Okay, so the assistant director will ask everyone to be quiet, and then the host will come out and do his little intro. And then he will introduce you one by one. When you hear your name, just walk to your station like we rehearsed, okay?"

Max nodded, even though she was talking to all of them and not really looking at him. She gave them a few more instructions before walking away to attend to a hundred different other details.

A moment later, the woman walked back up to Max and his mother.

"I have someone who wanted to wish you luck real quick."

She stepped aside, and Luca walked up to Max and his mom, grinning ear to ear.

"Dude, this is so rad!" he practically exploded.

It actually settled Max's bubbling stomach a little to see his best friend. Because that's what Luca was, and Max didn't feel weird anymore about thinking of him that way.

They bumped fists, and Max grinned back at him.

"You ready to kill it?" Luca asked.

"I'm ready to try, I guess."

"You're going to do *great*," his mom insisted, squeezing his shoulders.

A new thought seemed to light up Luca's face.

"Oh, man, guess what?" he said. "I didn't even get to tell you before you and your mom left. My dad got a new job!"

That took Max's mind off what was about to happen. His eyes went wide. He knew exactly how much that meant to Luca's family.

"Dude, that's so awesome! Doing what?"

"He's going to be a guard at this prison. It's crazy because he said he applied like a year ago and never heard anything. Then suddenly they called him."

Something about the word "prison" cut through Max's excitement for his friend, although he wasn't sure why at first.

"You know what else?" Luca continued. "It's the same jail Master Plan just got out of. My dad said when he went in for his introduction thing . . . orientation? Whatever. It was the same day they were releasing Master Plan. He actually got to *see* him walk out. With his own eyes. How cool, right? And how weird is that?"

Max didn't think it was weird at all. Luca didn't seem to make any connection between Master Plan being at that prison and his dad getting a new job there, even after Max told him about everything that had happened.

Max, however, knew enough by now to know nothing with Master Plan's name attached to it was ever an accident, or a coincidence.

He must have set it up. He *must* have.

But why? Why help Luca and his family? What would Master Plan get out of that? Luca had just told him the prison released Master Plan. He was free. He'd gotten what he wanted. He didn't need any help from a guard anymore, or Max.

Unless, Max thought, it was some kind of payment.

Could it really be Master Plan just doing something nice, to say thank you to Max?

He couldn't make himself believe that, but nothing else made sense to him in that moment.

Luca was still talking, not noticing Max's mind had

drifted. "Anyway, it's a really good job with good pay. My dad says everything is going to get better for us now, and I believe him."

"I'm really happy for you, dude," Max said, and he meant it. "You deserve it."

"Thanks. Hey, you know who else is here?" Luca asked him, sounding kind of freaked out but almost in a good way.

"Who?"

Luca pointed back at the block of the audience that made up the kids from their school.

Max squinted against the bright lights of the studio, into the sea of faces, many of which he recognized.

There was one that stood out almost immediately, though. Max's whole body suddenly felt cold, despite how hot it was in the studio.

It was Johnny Pro. He was actually there to watch Max compete.

Max expected to see hate in the older boy's eyes, and a hard look of revenge on his face.

Instead, Johnny Pro stared back at him with kind of a half grin on his lips.

Then, to Max's complete shock, his middle school tormentor gave him a nod, almost like he was encouraging Max to go out there and bake his best.

Max couldn't believe it. Were they cool now? After all that? After Max tossed him through a cake in front of practically the whole school?

It didn't make sense at first, but the more Max thought about it, and the more he looked back at the eighth grader, the more it kind of did make sense. Max realized that despite what he'd written to Master Plan, he was still thinking of the world too much like it was all heroes and villains.

Johnny Pro wasn't his nemesis. He was just a kid with a lot of anger inside of him, and maybe Max had shown him he couldn't just let that anger out on anyone he wanted and get away with it anymore. He hoped that was true, anyway.

If it wasn't, he'd just have to kick his butt again.

"Weird," he whispered to himself.

"Max?"

Max looked back at his best friend.

"You're my hero," Luca told him.

Max didn't know what to say to that.

Thankfully Luca smiled at him in a way that told Max Luca was just messing with him.

Max grinned again. "Oh, shut up, dude!"

Luca started laughing.

"Okay, I need you to go back to your seat, hon," the set

manager told him. "We're about to start."

"Good luck, dude!" Luca said, fist-bumping Max again before running back to the bleachers.

Max took a deep breath, letting it out slowly, trying to be calm.

He found he felt a little lighter. He really liked the idea that he and Johnny Pro could get past their problems, even after everything. Besides, he didn't *want* to have a nemesis. He didn't need an archenemy to battle.

Max knew now he also didn't need to be a superhero, as long as he was the hero of his own story.

He felt like that story was finally about to start.

ACKNOWLEDGMENTS

This is the part where I, the author, thank everyone who helped bring this book to life. I want to start by thanking the people I wrote this book for, the kids toughing it out through school every day, especially my fellow fat kids. I also want to thank every parent, teacher, bookseller, or librarian who put this book in the hands of one of those kids.

This book, just the initial idea for it, was a departure for me in pretty much every way, different from any other book I'd tried to write. As such, I'm grateful for the immediate and enthusiastic support of my longtime agent and friend, DongWon Song, and my wonderful editor, Ben Rosenthal, both of whom jumped right on board with the whole concept and helped me refine it into what it became. I also owe a spiritual debt of gratitude to the great Vincent D'Onofrio, whose performance as Kingpin on the Netflix Daredevil series provided the first grain of inspiration for this novel. I don't think it would exist without him.

I wouldn't be here, or writing, without the continued support of my family. My wife, Nikki, is the center of my whole universe. My mother, Barbara, is the most ardent supporter and volunteer publicist any author could have. All my cousins and nieces and nephews who make me want to write books for kids like them. I also want to thank my adopted family at the Doghouse Pro-Wrestling Club in Queens, NYC, who helped me find the kind of confidence as a kid that I hope this book helps other kids find.

My thanks also to the authors who read and supported this book early, such as the great Julie Murphy, another definite inspiration, Chuck Wendig, Mur Lafferty, John David Anderson, and librarian and editor Angie Manfredi. All the folks at Katherine Tegen Books and HarperCollins Children's who have helped and continue to help shepherd my middle-grade novels have my eternal gratitude: publicist Lauren Levite, assistant editor Tanu Srivastava, production editor Laura Harshberger, managing editor Mark Rifkin, as well as designers Andrea Vandergrift and Joel Tippie, production manager Kristen Eckhardt, and cover artist Kat Fajardo. It takes a village that is also a circus that is also an elite ragtag team of warriors from the future to raise a book. Finally, I want to thank Katherine Tegen herself. None of us would be here without her.